# HORROR UNIVERSITY

ALSO BY KEVIN CERAGNO

*Troubled Lives*

# HORROR UNIVERSITY

A Novel

———◆———

KEVIN CERAGNO

Full Court Press
Englewood Cliffs, New Jersey

Published in the United States of America
by Full Court Press, 601 Palisade Avenue,
Englewood Cliffs, NJ 07632
*fullcourtpressnj.com*

ISBN 978-1-938812-98-9
Library of Congress Catalog No. 2017945519

*Editing and book design by Barry Sheinkopf for Bookshapers
(bookshapers.com)*

TO MY MOTHER, FATHER, AND SISTER

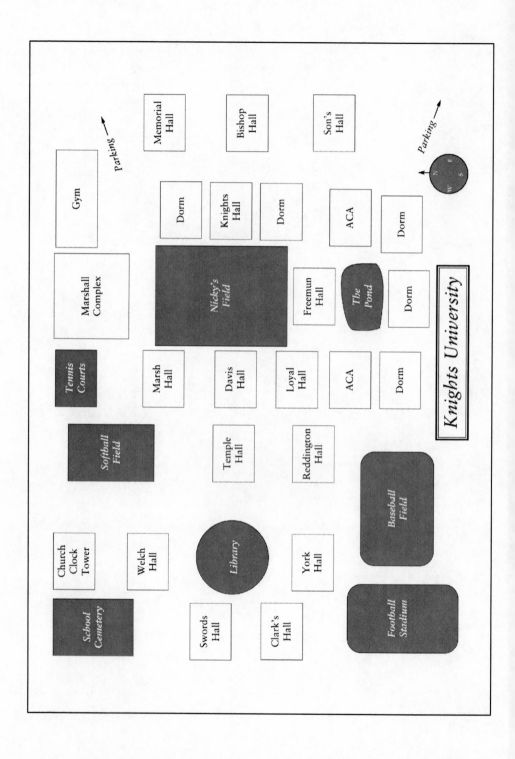

Knights University

# CHAPTER 1

S WINGING HER REAR END in tight jeans as she turned down the empty sidewalk under a windless night sky, twenty-two-year-old Rachel Yards heard three guys gawk at her from across a deserted field on the otherwise quiet campus. The college senior lowered her head, but a smile played over her smooth lips. She jogged up the concrete steps of Knights Hall, a four-story gothic building dominated by two towers. A sudden gust from behind pressed her wavy, black hair against her neck.

Heading up four flights of stairs to the radio station, her heels echoed on the poorly lit stairway, her perfume in a losing struggle with the dank smell of the building. Halfway down the hallway, the hip-hop music from behind a brown door, with *Radio Station* in bright red letters above it, was already getting louder. She entered a room packed with CD players, turntables, computers, control panels, and speakers. On the side walls, the shelves were filled with hundreds of CDs, LPs, and cassettes. She waved to a friend, Mark Lexington, another senior, who was wearing headphones and sitting below a lit-up *On the Air* sign.

He ran his fingers over his brown goatee by way of reply.

She raised her eyebrows at him, pointing to a spiral notebook she'd come to pick up from a cluttered table. The neon light in the room made her brown eyes glow more than usual. It also high-lighted her long eyelashes.

He nodded, thinking again of how many times he'd wanted to date her. Since freshman year, they had shared a love of music and radio; the former running back wished there could be more. He gave her a thumbs-up in response to the note she'd just written: *How's it going?*

With the notebook in hand, she blew him a kiss goodbye.

Almost every Sunday afternoon, when she played Pearl Jam, Nirvana, and other grunge rockers, he visited her. With a sigh, he introduced the next song.

On the last flight of stairs, scratching behind her right ear, Rachel knocked off an earring that bounced on the steps. "Oh, *damn* it!" she exclaimed as the earring fell into the stairwell and landed on the floor below street level. The stairs ended at the mouth of a dark hallway. She'd never been down there. Her black hair fell across her face as she kneeled to pick up the earring and slipped it into her pocket. She had left her purse in her dorm. She'd heard the old library was there. Rachel began to rub her forearms. "For sure, the heat doesn't reach here," she giggled.

She liked the darkness.

Mystery charmed her.

A couple of steps later, she started to run her fingers along the tiled wall. Unable to see anything in front of her and about to turn around, her hand fell against a door. Moments later, when her eyes adjusted, she could see the sign: *Library*. As she grabbed the cold door knob, a chill shot down her spine. The door creaked open; her body shook.

The Jersey native was about to return to the stairs when a glowing yellow light at the other end of the room drew her in. A long, narrow aisle lined with overstuffed bookcases led ahead, ending at another bookshelf perpendicular to the rest.

On her third step, she heard the door behind her close. She held her breath, expecting a bogeyman to appear, but nothing happened. She kept moving further in, every so often touching books covered in years of dust. The strange yellow light drew her forward like a magnet. She wiped the dust on her jeans.

Her angled eyebrows rose, and goose bumps broke out, when she thought she heard a humming noise of human origin.

The humming soon grew louder, the light brighter.

When her fingers reached the bookcase at the end of the aisle, she laid the notebook on the dusty floor. Peering between the volumes, Rachel wanted to scream, but she knew that, if she did, she'd be dead. To stop shaking, she pressed her hands against the spines of the books.

On the other side of the last bookcase, twenty feet ahead, a motionless, heavy-set boy lay naked on a wooden table, his wrists and ankles chained to four posts. Candles were spread out all over the floor. Between the bookshelf and the boy, the legend *K & T* had been inscribed on the floor. Hovering over him stood a group of five people, dressed in brown robes that hid much of their heads; their faces were covered with white masks. They had hammers, saws, screwdrivers, and scalpels in their fists.

Rachel took a step back, bringing her hands to her nose and mouth. Moments later, she began to sniffle. The dust on her fingers and palms brought more terror to her oval face. Perspiration had cooled her cheeks. Before she could take another step backward, she sneezed.

A tall man, firmly gripping a butcher knife in his hands near the prisoner's chin, called out, "*What?* Who dares?"

Back-peddling, Rachel fell onto her rear end. She rolled to her left, sprang up to her hands and knees, and pulled on one of the shelves.

"Go!" The man pointed with the knife. "Get the intruder!"

Sprinting down the path, crying the entire way, Rachel soon heard footsteps behind her. When she reached the door, she twisted and turned the knob, but it wouldn't move. Her eyes widened. Remembering it had opened into the room, the girl leaned back and it swung open. Turning right, she ran down the dark hall to the stairway. At the first step, she kicked off her heels and continued running, not looking back.

A whistling wind greeted her once she bolted outside. Two squirrels chasing each another across the pavement made her turn left. As she neared the concrete steps, she thought she saw one of her hooded pursuers in the arch of the unused door. Screaming like mad, Rachel took the steps two at a time. No one heard her. Once on the sidewalk that circled the field, she extended her arm, grabbed the top bar of the iron fence, and flung her legs over it, but she tumbled onto her hands and knees. In seconds, she was running again, heart beating in terror.

After what seemed like forever, she reached the other end of Nicky's Field, where she tried to jump over the fence the same way as before. This time, her legs hit the post, twisting her body, and she fell hard on her back. She grunted, forced herself up, and dashed across the street to the nearest dormitory. Pounding on the door of Marsh Hall, she yelled, "*Open up*! Someone *help* me, *please*! Open."

The door swung open, and two tall, drunken seniors, plastic cups of beer in their hands, asked, "Rachel! Where ya been?"

She grabbed a cup from the hand of the guy on her left as she zoomed past them. Near another set of doors, shaking uncontrollably, feet burning, she drank the beer, most of which ran down her flat chin onto her black top. "Where? Where's the party?"

The guy who'd lost his beer said, "Second floor."

She sprinted up the stairs, barefoot.

The guys smiled at each other and laughed. One winked. "That's my kind of woman."

# CHAPTER 2

On Friday, Rachel was stirring a bowl of chicken soup two rows from a wall composed mostly of windows that let plenty of sunlight into the noisy Marshall Complex cafeteria. Her roommate Stephanie Brooks' blue eyes widened when their eyes met. "Look who finally got out of bed."

The pretty blonde with the straight, even features, forehead covered by bangs, and small glasses took a seat opposite her. "That was some party." They'd met freshman year in a communications class and often spoke about setting up their own radio station one day.

Rachel smiled. "Yes, it was." She took a spoonful of soup.

"Ladies!" Mark Lexington exclaimed as he swung around the wooden table to sit next to Rachel, setting down a red tray with a steaming cheeseburger, fries, and a Coke.

Stephanie giggled. "Rachel, you were so unusually quiet, it was like you'd seen a ghost."

Rachel wiped her mouth with a napkin. "You can say that."

Cheeseburger inches from his mouth, Mark asked, "Yeah—

Rach, what the hell happened to you last night? When I saw you at the station, you were your usual feisty self. But at the party you looked completely wrecked. You get into a fight and lose?" He bit into his sandwich.

Larry Moore, whose hazel eyes were an abrupt contrast to his black hair, a senior deejay and reporter for the *University Times*, had just sat down at the table with a hot dog and onions. "You *were* a mess at the party," he agreed. "No offense."

Rachel remained unresponsive.

Larry turned to Stephanie, her thin eyebrows raised. ". . . Rachel," she asked, "is there something you're not telling us?"

Rachel sat up straight. "I. . .um, well, I kinda stumbled onto a human sacrifice at the old library."

"A *what*?" Mark began choking.

Slapping his back, Rachel asked, "Better?"

He smiled and, with a napkin, wiped ketchup and bread off his mouth.

Rachel took another spoonful of soup and leaned closer to the others. "I saw men in brown robes with masks on their faces. And a chubby kid, naked, chained to. . . . I don't know if he was dead or alive."

"You're kidding, right?" Stephanie had leaned back in her seat.

Rachel cleared her throat. "Ah, no. Back behind the dusty stacks of the old Library. They had a circle of candles. And I saw these men dressed like monks, with white masks on their faces and knives and stuff in their hands. They were circling this naked kid, chained, like I said, to these posts." She took a sip of ginger ale. "I-I kicked up some dust and. . .sneezed. That stopped them. They chased after me, but I outran them. I lost my heels on the stairs."

She took another spoonful of soup.

The others looked at each other in silence.

Mark turned to her. "...What—uh, what were you doing down there anyway?" His brown eyes had become razor sharp.

She poked him in the ribs. "After I saw you at the station, my earring popped off and it fell down the stairwell. I'd gone after it when I came across a door marked *Library*. I just went inside. And then...then this glowing light seemed to pull me in. Must've been the candles." She scooped up a big piece of chicken from the soup.

While Larry and Stephanie sat there with their mouths open, Mark took a meditative bite of his burger. "Sounds like you had a nightmare after too many beers."

Rachel shook her head. "No. It's the truth. . . ." She studied the lousy job she'd done on her fingernails. "Don't we have an exam in English today?"

"Rachel—" Stephanie had leaned in even closer, adjusting her glasses— "have you told anyone else? It's totally bizarre. You sure that's what you saw?"

Rachel smiled. "You're the first ones I'm telling, as usual. Have I ever lied to you before? Yeah. It was pretty wild. And of *course* I'm sure. That K & T was right there on the floor."

Larry picked at his tooth. "K & T? Sounds like some hard-edge fraternity."

Stephanie leaned back. "Rachel. We joined you swimming in Freemun's Pond. We had a party in the station. We set up our own miniature golf course on Nicky's Field, but—"

Mark snapped his fingers. "You know, I've heard rumors about a secret group on campus that keeps outsiders out. Maybe this guy was one of them." He chewed on a fry and thought about it. "My brother mentioned there were ghosts roaming Davis Hall when he attended here a couple of years ago. He also told me about a suspicious fire in Bishop Hall during a Young Democrats meeting. Luckily, no one was hurt, but that destroyed the membership in that group. Could it be that somehow, some way, they're connected?" He wolfed down another fry. "You know, they say they filmed part of *The Omen* here."

"Really?" Larry's boxy face turned white. "What part?"

"When the nanny jumps off the ledge to hang herself?"

Stephanie ran a hand along her slender neck.

Larry asked, "But aren't those ghosts supposedly, like, old professors or something?"

Mark shrugged.

"And weren't there flyers around campus weeks ago," Stephanie whispered, "about a freshman girl who disappeared?"

"You think," Larry asked, "you think those people Rachel saw last night have something to do with *that*?"

Stephanie would not let go of her neck. "Shouldn't we speak to campus security?"

Larry frowned. "It's all heresy."

Rachel pushed her tray away. "We all know the clock tower story, don't we?"

The guys grew quiet; Stephanie slid her chair forward.

Rachel whispered, "The wind was blowing one rainy night. Lightning bolts, loudest thunder you ever heard. The campus was deserted. Up in the old church tower, some history professor had documents explaining who'd actually founded this school. It wasn't the late governor's nephew, but, supposedly, a 'secret society.'" She gestured at Stephanie. "With *Mafia* money. The professor had hidden the papers somewhere in the clock tower. They trapped him up there. When he refused to hand them over, he was stabbed to death, and his body was hung on the clock at two minutes to midnight." The guys were still hunched over, Stephanie had her hands over her mouth. "To this day, no one has found those papers. And *he's* believed to be one of those ghosts. . . . His name was Gordon Cunningham."

Mark put up his index finger to his thick nose. "Let me guess. At that time every night. . .the bell chimes."

Rachel smiled. "Actually, the bells chime once a year in May. The murder happened decades ago."

"Next month," whispered Stephanie behind her fingers.

Larry asked, "Who told you that story?"

"My uncle Freddie," said Rachel, "who graduated from here in 1980."

Stephanie elbowed Larry's bicep. "He's the one who took Rachel and me gambling in Atlantic City at Caesars sophomore year."

Glancing at his watch, Larry announced, "We're going to be late for class."

"Wait." Mark grabbed Rachel's small hand. "Let's *all* go down to the old library tonight."

"Okay." Larry nodded. "Seeing is believing."

Turning to her right, Stephanie cleared her throat and said, "If isn't The Tree and Fatso."

A tall, slim girl with a long face and brown hair said, "Playing in the mud again, Rachel? With beer all over you! I've never seen you look so foolish."

"No shoes? How tacky!" her much shorter companion added,

blue eyes full of contempt, grinding her teeth in a wide mouth in a round face bordered by dirty-blonde hair. "Shaking like you ran a marathon. What else did you do before—"

Approaching from further up and on the other side of the table, two guys wearing black T shirts with *Knights University* in white letters on their chests and matching hats, started cheering, "Rachel! Last night, last. . . ! Rachel Yards! You are the *man*! You are the *man*!" They gave her high fives.

Excited but confused, Rachel asked, "I'm the *man*? Is that a compliment?"

Together, the three answered, "For you, Rachel. Yes!"

The round girl stuck her pudgy index finger into her mouth. Heads down, they escaped deeper into the cafeteria.

LATER ON IN REDDINGTON HALL, on the last question of her English exam, Rachel gazed up at the glass-paneled door and saw a guy of medium build. "Oh, my God!" she gasped out loud.

Her classmates looked at her.

At the whiteboard, tall and portly Charlie Wells, who had been looking out the window, turned to her, marker in his hand, salt-and-pepper hair resting on his prominent ears. "Miss Yards? Something you'd like to share with the class?"

"N-No."

"Then button it up until you finish your exam!"

The other three, sitting in the same row, shared looks.

Ten minutes later, when everyone else had laid their exam books on Dr. Wells' desk, the three stopped her near the door. "What'd you see in the hallway?" Mark asked.

Rachel heaved her books up against her chest. "A guy in slacks, wearing a white mask just like those monks."

"*What?*"

Turning to Wells, Rachel asked, "Dr. Wells, are there any secret societies on campus?"

"You're crazy, sweetheart," Mark whispered.

The professor hoisted his pants. "Miss Yards, this institution was founded over a hundred years ago by the governor's family to educate and train young men and women to better themselves intellectually and establish productive careers. We have students from all fifty states attending here. Rumors of secret societies, Mafia money, ghosts. . .they're simply awful, and they should have died out long ago." He coughed when she, wearing a knee-length skirt, stepped onto the dais and bumped into him. "And if you allow yourself to be seduced by such claims, Miss Yards, you'd better re-examine your philosophy of life."

"She will. She will." The blonde had grabbed Rachel by her upper arm and was already dragging her out of the room.

In the hallway, Mark grumbled, "Why did you ask him that?"

She laid her hand on his chest. "If anyone knows about secret societies, it's him."

Mark shook his head, knowing she'd study the subject to death.

Larry tapped his books. "Come on. Let's go. We got Powers of the FCC in Davis." He hated being late to class, especially in communications. "I can just see the headlines now," he added dryly, "'*Secret Society. . . .*'" They left with Rachel in the lead.

Moments later, Dr. Wells had closed the classroom door, sat down at the desk, and pulled out his cell phone. He punched in a number. "Henry? Charlie. We may have a problem. Rachel Yards just asked me whether secret societies exist on campus."

"What?"

"We need to talk."

"Midnight, in my office.  Be careful."

Wells turned off his cell, replaced it in his briefcase, and offered up a short prayer before he left the classroom in a hurry.

# CHAPTER 3

STEPHANIE CLUTCHED THE VERTICAL FRAME of the doorway at the bottom of the Knights Hall stairs as tightly as she could. "We have to go in *there?* It's so quiet, so dark and narrow. Can't we do this some other time?"

Larry clicked on his flashlight. "The sooner we get this over with the better."

"Don't be such a scaredy-cat," Rachel said as she slipped between them and headed into the darkness with her flashlight.

"Rach!" Mark called out. "Wait up."

Stephanie began to rub her arms. "I'm glad I wore this long-sleeved top. It's cold down here."

Larry, who was next to her, asked, "How far down's the library, Rachel?" Their flashlights were falling on tiled walls, the floor, the unlit fluorescent fixtures, and two doors on the right, the one closest to them marked *Janitor*.

Rachel turned a moment. "About halfway down to the left."

Adjusting her glasses, Stephanie asked, "What made you keep going down here, alone, in the dark?"

"Curiosity." Rachel was brushing black strands of hair from her face.

"I never gave this place much thought." Mark swung his flashlight across an enormous hanging spider web.

"Here we are." Rachel directed her flashlight on the sign that read *Library*.

Larry reached for the knob. "It's locked." He glanced at Rachel's face, partially bathed in light. "I think your secret society wised up."

"No problem." She held up a small pocket knife. "Mark, can you take this, sweetie?" She handed him her flashlight and dropped to her knees to pick the lock. After a few twists and turns of the blade, she heard a click and pushed open the door with a creak. "There ya go." She took the flashlight. "Last one in. . . ."

"Allow me." Mark stepped in front of her into the room.

She rested her hand on his shoulder, followed by Stephanie and Larry, the tallest of the four.

They all gasped once their eyes adjusted to the dark and their flashlights swept the room left and right. Larry went on, "Look at all the books. Rows and rows and rows of 'em." This time there was no glowing light or humming sound to distract anyone.

"Wait." Mark lifted a heavy textbook off a shelf. "Let's keep the door open with this."

"Good idea," Larry murmured.

Mark motioned to Rachel with his flashlight. She went off at her usual stride toward the center of the room.

"Hold on." Mark grabbed her by her belt. "This is a first for most of us down here."

In a tighter group, they moved up the center aisle, not saying a word.

Stephanie sneezed. "Sorry. The dust."

Larry whispered, "Okay. Let's go."

Swinging beams of light across the floor, the bookshelves, the high ceiling, they neared the spot where Rachel had halted the night before. The dust looked like gray blankets.

"Why doesn't the school use this—"

Larry pulled Stephanie backwards, index finger on his lips.

Rachel tapped a bookshelf. "My notebook's gone." She shone the light where she had last seen it. "They know my play list for Sunday."

Stephanie shook her head.

Mark wiped sweat off his high forehead. "Where did you see these monks in the robes?"

Rachel pointed. "On the other side of this shelf."

Larry waved them on. He crept along the shelf, directing the flashlight at the floor. Sweat began to form near his ears. He turned at the end of the aisle, expecting robes, white masks, and glittering knives, but found only more bookshelves.

"No." Rachel raised her voice. "The K & T were inscribed right there on the floor." She pointed to a rug under a bookshelf. "Over there was the wooden table with the kid chained to the posts. There were candles all around here." She moved the beam of light in a circle. "I can still smell the scent."

Larry and Mark shook their heads; Stephanie took a deep breath and held it, as if she were doing yoga.

Mark said, "I must admit, the rug seems odd."

"What do you want to do?" Larry asked. "See what's under it?"

Rachel retraced their steps, turned right, and moved over two aisles, followed by Stephanie. "What's this?"

When the guys reached them, the two girls had their flashlights set on the floor near a bookshelf. "Bloodstains?"

The two guys looked at each other. "The rug."

They returned to the center bookshelf.

At the edge of the brown carpet, Stephanie asked, "How the hell are we going to move that?"

"By taking out these books." Mark put the flashlight behind him, aimed at the task at hand. "You two." He pointed at the girls. "Go on the other side."

Stephanie remarked, "There's not much dust on these compared to the rest."

Once four rows of philosophy and theology texts had been removed, Mark said, "Larry and I'll push the shelf. You and Steph pull it."

The girls nodded.

They grunted with the effort, and their feet began to slip and slide, but the bookcase refused to move.

"Shit!" Rachel swung her arms downward and hit the edge of one of the shelves with both fists, causing it to vibrate out of its brackets.

The four gasped and crouched on hands and knees. The guys slid the bottom shelf out toward them and placed it to their right, near Larry's pile. The two pulled the rug up. Below it, a cursive *K & T* became visible.

"Dear God." Mark pulled the rug higher.

*Whap!*

"What was that?" Stephanie had whipped her head around.

"It's the *door!*" Rachel got to her feet and ran down the aisle empty-handed.

Mark yelled, "Rachel! Wait!"

Stephanie charged after her with her flashlight. "Don't leave me!"

Moving the other shelf to the floor, Mark said, "Fearless Rachel." He and Larry ran after the girls with their flashlights.

When they reached the door, Stephanie turned to them. "Larry! We're locked in. What are we gonna do?"

He hugged her. "Calm down."

Rachel leaned on Mark. "There must be a window or another door somewhere."

"Let's go back to the K & T and make a right turn," said Mark. When they got there, he added, "Rachel? Your flashlight's gone."

"Let's move."

Rachel pointed. "Straight ahead. A door."

They ran up to it.

"*Damn.*" Larry pounded on the door. "It's bolted shut. Where the hell do you think it led to?"

Stephanie mumbled, "Probably an exit."

Rachel pointed to a passage on her right. "What's that?"

They took it, but it ended at a brick wall. "Dead end." Larry cursed. "Shit."

"There must be a secret passage." Rachel started running her fingers over the bricks.

"Rachel," Larry exclaimed, "don't be ridiculous."

Rachel screamed, "I just saw a hooded monk run by!"

A humming noise rose behind them.

Stephanie reached for Larry. "What's that?"

Rachel gulped, "That's what I heard last night!"

Larry cleared his throat. "Look! I see a yellow light moving toward us."

They dashed to the wall.

Mark said, "There are no windows."

"Must've sealed 'em."

Above and to her right, Rachel spotted a foot-long statue of a gargoyle attached to the wall. When she twisted its angry mouth, a section of the wall sprang open with a hiss. "Holy Moly."

Stephanie was astonished, too. "What *is* this? A movie?"

"Move! *Move!*" Larry ordered. They plunged through the opening, two at a time, hand in hand. When Larry and Stephanie had squeezed through, the wall slid shut, forcing them to the cold floor.

Rachel asked, "You two all right?"

"Yeah." Larry helped Stephanie to her feet. *"Go."*

Running through the narrow tunnel, aided by flashlights, Stephanie gasped, "Where do these doors lead to? I hope no one pops out of 'em. What is this place? This wasn't on Orientation." They were on an incline.

Between breaths, Rachel said, "We'll check it out next time we come here."

Mark glared at her.

Moments later, they were confronted by a huge, brown iron door bolted in the middle and bottom; two small windows at the top allowed moonlight to pour into the tunnel in two diagonal beams.

When Rachel regained her breath, she said to Mark, "Pick me up so I can look out the windows."

He wrapped his arms around her legs just below her rear end and lifted her up about a foot.

"Holy *shit!*" she shrieked. "I can see Nicky's Field." She tapped his head. "Put me down!" He set her down, and she used her pocket knife to fiddle with the bolt.

Candlelight and humming noises were rapidly approaching from behind them.

Stephanie jumped. "Hurry, Rachel."

A click quieted everyone down; another click got their blood pumping.

The footsteps and voices grew louder.

They all pulled on the vertical handle, which caused the door to spring open. "That was too easy," Larry said. "The school supposedly never uses this." They lunged outside into a gust of wind and slammed the door.

They said nothing until Larry heard a crumpling noise coming from the top of the building. "Take cover." Chunks of stone were falling.

"Rachel!" Mark pushed her to the ground and threw himself over her.

Once the dust settled, Larry, holding Stephanie, came over to Rachel and Mark. "You guys all right?"

Shaking in Larry's arms, Stephanie said, "That wasn't an accident."

When Mark pulled himself and Rachel up, he asked, "Everybody okay?"

Wiping gravel off, Rachel nodded. "Thanks. . . . The school should fix that."

"Yeah, Rach." Fists clenched, Stephanie added, "Call Maintenance about it."

They hurried down the steps with five pairs of eyes watching them.

# CHAPTER 4

ALONE AT MIDNIGHT AT HIS DESK in a spacious, green-carpeted office in Temple Hall, President of the University Henry O'Connor was filling out a form for the upcoming graduation when he heard a knock at the door.

"Come in," he said. A desk lamp, and two candles on the coffee table between his desk and chairs, provided the only light, aside from the glow of his computer screen on a credenza near the window closest to him. In the corner, a clock radio was playing Beethoven. He lowered his glasses down the bridge of his straight nose and watched Professor Wells close the door behind him. "Right on time as usual. Take a seat. Be with you in a minute." Two more lines of information, and the application was complete. O'Connor's computer-generated signature was already on the form. "Talk to me, Charlie." He took off the glasses attached to a chain around his neck, which was distinguished by a prominent Adam's apple.

Sinking his bulk into the armchair, Wells muttered, "It wasn't until the end of class that Rachel Yards asked me about secret societies. I gave her the usual speech." He shook his head. "I heard she was scared out of her mind." He glanced at the packed bookcases.

The wrinkles on O'Connor's face grew more pronounced as he studied the separate piles of paperwork on his desk. "How much does she know?"

Wells sat up. "I'm not sure. I overheard her mention to her friends that she'd seen a guy wearing a white mask in the hallway. But they didn't seem as convinced as she was."

O'Connor rubbed his eyes. "I've been here for almost thirty years, and we've never had a problem. All this for a lousy notebook." He shook his head. "Keep an eye on her. She's a wild creature. I've heard her on the station. . . . And people would notice if she disappeared, unlike the others."

Wells scratched the fringe of remaining hair on the back of his head. "Henry, hasn't this. . .gone too far?"

O'Connor pounded his desk with a force that shook the certificates on the wall near the shaded windows. "Of *course* it has, but some people don't know when to stop. Power in the hands of a few is dangerous. And the information in that clock tower could destroy many lives." He caressed his lined forehead. "A loose cannon like her has to be *scared* somehow. See to it."

Wells rose, hitching his pants at the waistline, perspiration forming at his temples. "Absolutely. I'll keep you informed."

"Careful, Charlie. We're walking a fine line here." O'Connor took a deep breath. "We have to think of the good of the university, but we have to watch our own asses. And hers."

Near the door, the twenty-four-year veteran nodded. "Thanks, Henry. I'll watch my back." He opened the door and left.

O'Connor rolled his chair on the plastic mat to the computer behind his desk, clicked to an article about the disappearance of another college student three weeks before, and closed his eyes, wondering which misfit would be next.

IN ANOTHER PART OF CAMPUS, sitting in the dark on the floor near his bed on the third floor of Swords Hall, Larry whispered, "Stephanie's right. Like that cement block just happened to fall when we left the building. And that door. I've heard it's never used, but it opened so easily."

Across from him, Rachel smiled. "Hey, Larry! Earlier, you were acting like a doubting Thomas."

Larry raised his eyebrows. "Not after what *we* just saw."

Resting his back next to Rachel against the drawers of his desk, Mark asked, "Who do you think's involved?"

"Wells."

A chill ran through Stephanie's body. "You really want to go back? Shouldn't we go to the cops?"

Rachel crossed her legs at the ankles. "And tell them *what* exactly? We gotta find what's behind those doors."

Mark cleared his throat. "She's got a point, though, Rach. Even this is pretty odd in a university."

"Tomorrow at noon, then," Rachel said. "We'll go to the police. Tell them what we know and ask them to investigate. Later we'll do some research at the library. We can search for books and check the Internet for secret societies."

"Sounds good."

Rachel leaned back, and silence fell. They were still breathing heavily. Since it was the weekend, many students had left the campus, making it feel like a ghost town.

". . .Why?" Larry murmured.

"Why what?"

"Why are they *doing* these things?" he asked, grinding his teeth. "And how long's it been going on for?"

"Money. Power. Control. Who knows? How long is anybody's guess!" Rachel leaned sideways against Mark, who put his arm around her waist. "That's what we're going to find out."

Five minutes after Rachel and Stephanie fell asleep, the door to their room in Clarks Hall slowly creaked open. Five figures in brown robes, with white masks on their faces, slipped in. They were carrying knives, rope, duct tape, a hypodermic syringe, and a long rod. Their combined mass did not allow much light to enter from the hallway. The last one carefully closed the door. Two people moved to their right toward Stephanie; the rest huddled around Rachel's bed. As the lead monk, the one with a butcher knife, placed his left hand on Rachel's mouth, the others tied her wrists and ankles to the bed posts. Although he waved the knife in front of her, she continued to struggle and squirm.

The previous summer at Seaside Heights, New Jersey, Rachel had fought off a mugger, with a patch over his left eye, who tried to rob her with a knife after she had been taught by her brothers, causing the hoodlum to flee.

Across the room, one monk covered Stephanie's mouth while the fifth rubbed her bare arm with an alcohol swab. Seconds after he plunged the syringe into the side of her shoulder, she was sleeping like a baby. They joined the others at Rachel's bed.

Kneeling on top of her at her hips, the leader ran the knife along her throat. Two pieces of duct tape now covered her mouth. The others hovered over the half-naked girl spread-eagle on the bed below a shaded window.

"Ms. Yards," the master said. "You are good. Twice you've escaped. But now you have foolishly involved your friends."

She kept squirming, terror flickering in her eyes.

He seized her by the hair. "Since you're too well known on campus to vanish, we've chosen another strategy. You see, sweetheart. . . ." He started to cut off the buttons on the long-sleeved shirt she used as pajamas.

She blinked.

The others began to hum.

"Our little group—" he cut down to the third button, revealing half of her breasts— "has been around for a very long time." He reached halfway down her shirt. "Doing some very important things for this university, academically, financially, socially." Two more buttons, and he would have the entire shirt open. "And we're not going to stop because of a beautiful, pain-in-the-ass *bitch*." He rubbed her stomach and breasts with his plastic glove.

She closed her eyes and turned her head away.

He reached behind him for her legs. "You are a beauty. Just the kind we like at this school." He climbed off her and was handed a branding iron. "Therefore, we're going to leave you with this message—-to remind you to shut up and to stay out of our business."

She was rocking back and forth on the bed.

The others held her down.

He lifted the rod up above her stomach. "This might hurt a bit." A glowing red *K & T* appeared on the bottom of it. "Quiet, Rachel."

She screamed, twisting against the sheets.

*"Rachel. Rachel!"*

Rachel opened her eyes. Stephanie was standing over her. "What's wrong? Talk to me."

Quieting down, wrapped up like a mummy, Rachel said, "I had a nightmare." She loosened the sheets and fell asleep.

In her nightgown, Stephanie shook the bed. *"Rachel*! Nightmare about what? Tonight? Say something." She heard a snore by way of reply. "My God. She's unbelievable."

# CHAPTER 5

S ITTING AT A LIBRARY COMPUTER on Saturday along with a row of others, Rachel typed in *secret societies* and clicked *Search*. As the donut started spinning, she burped. "I just tasted the pizza we had."

"Rachel! That's disgusting." Stephanie shoved her shoulder. "You're worse than a guy." She adjusted her glasses. ". . .You know, that tall, dark, handsome Sergeant Dolan with the really dark brown eyes, almost black, and that demonic-sounding voice wasn't exactly thrilled with us. So he takes our names and fills out some paperwork, so what? They arrested that guy last night, they think the case is closed. . . . They found the bodies—you know, those two students from here. Probably runaways who couldn't handle the pressure of attending a major university."

Stephanie smiled. "He *did* mention that he'd graduated from here. Double major in criminal justice and medieval history."

Ignoring her, and the news of the day that flashed on the screen (*Serial Killer Gus Clement, a.k.a. the Woodsman Killer, Captured near Knights University in Rockland County, New York. A Suspect in Ten Murders*), Rachel gazed out the windows. The sun had again disappeared behind the clouds.

Behind them, arms crossed, Mark and Larry shook their heads.

Moments later, paragraphs of information and a list of names appeared on the screen, accompanied by descriptions. Rachel asked, "You think there's a Skull & Bones here?"

Larry leaned toward her. "Probably not. That's Yale."

She pointed at the middle of the screen. "Knights Templar."

Stephanie grabbed her roommate's arm. "*K & T.*"

Rachel read out loud: "'They carried swords, wore white cloaks with a red cross on the chest, and carried a white shield with a red cross. At the onset of the Crusades, the Knights Templar were established to protect travelers. As the order grew in numbers and strength, it was tasked with protecting sensitive documents from the Holy Land. The Knights built castles and created a monetary system that was the predecessor of bank certificates and credit cards. Centuries later, the Church, seeing the order as a dangerous rival, brutally crushed it on Friday, October 13, 1307.'"

Stephanie jumped to her feet. "Friday the 13th!"

Rachel read on. "'Knights who escaped joined other secret societies or became pirates.'"

The four looked at the windows to see birds flying past the building.

Mark said, "They're not the guys *you* saw."

"Or dreamed about."

". . .What?" Mark looked down at Rachel.

She turned to Stephanie with raised eyebrows.

"Here's one. . .the Assassins." Stephanie began to absently twist a strand of her long blonde hair. "Another group from the Holy

Land."

Larry said, "Those robed *guys* sure acted like assassins."

Rachel smiled. "Priory of Sion. That's Leonardo Da Vinci's group! The Rosicrucians had Sir Francis Bacon as a member."

At the foot of the aisle, a heavy-set woman cleared her throat. "Quiet, please. This is a library."

Rachel scrolled down. "Freemasons." She tapped her fingernails on the screen. "Included George Washington, Alexander Hamilton, Benjamin Franklin, Paul Revere, John Adams, Thomas Jefferson. . . .Henry Ford, J. Edgar Hoover. . . ."

"Look—the symbol's on the back of a dollar bill," Mark pointed out. "The all-seeing eye above the pyramid."

The sunlight that reappeared through the windows and fell across the banks of computers couldn't lighten the raven darkness of Rachel's hair.

Stephanie pushed the keyboard in front of her closer to the monitor. "They never mentioned secret societies in *high* school."

"The Illuminati!" Rachel popped up in her seat, forcing Mark back. "'They believed in 'earth, fire, air, and water.' And they were always in conflict with the Church.' They sound like those monks we ran into across campus."

Scrolling down, Rachel muttered, "Council of Foreign Relations?"

Larry said, "The CFR publishes *Foreign Affairs* magazine. My father has been reading *FA* for years."

"Really?" Mark raised his eyebrows.

Rubbing the back of his hand across his face, Larry said, "Secret societies were composed of inventors, scientists, protectors, men who believed in open government." He stared at the Oxford dictionaries on the bookshelves next to the windows. "This is a different type of secret society."

"What is all this talk about secret societies?" Professor Wells asked as he came down the aisle. "Miss Yards, I'm sure *you're* the driving force behind this meeting of the minds."

Rachel tapped Mark's knee, and he helped her move her chair back. She shifted to her left and crossed one leg over the other in her blue shorts. "What were you saying, Professor Wells?"

The tall man coughed. "What. . .uh, what's your fascination with secret societies?" he asked with an effort at seriousness.

She raised her angled eyebrows. "I ran across—"

"*The Da Vinci Code*," Stephanie exclaimed, covering Rachel's mouth. "She's fascinated by it, and *National Treasure*, the Nicolas Cage flick? She's thinking of writing her final paper on secret societies."

Mark had begun to squeeze Rachel's shoulder.

The man scratched his balding head. "That so?"

"Yes."

"Good. But you won't find any secret societies on *this* campus." One last glance at her legs, and he left.

When Stephanie could no longer see him in the Reference Room, she hit the desk. "Damn it, Rachel. You were chewing my hand."

"Sorry. Let's check for students who disappeared recently." Rachel's hands flew over the keyboard. ". . .Huh. Nothing."

Mark rubbed his weather-beaten lips. "Type in the school's name and the name of the student."

Larry had meanwhile grown thoughtful. "How did he know to find us here?" he asked.

Mark shrugged. "Probably the bossy librarian told him."

As Rachel typed away, Stephanie was licking her palm.

A rumble emerged from the high ceiling. "Someone turn on the air conditioner?" Mark grabbed his extended ear lobes.

Rachel clapped. "Got it!"

They gathered closer to the screen. She began to read out loud: "'Sarah Appleton disappeared three weeks ago. She graduated tops in her class from an all-girl catholic high school in Connecticut.'"

The screen began to flicker.

Stephanie shivered. "They're trying to freeze us out!"

Rachel clicked on another link. "Melvin Nill disappeared last week. He disputed Darwinism—what the. . . ?"

An error message had appeared in the middle of the screen. She sat up, bumping the back of her head into Mark's chest, and clicked the *OK* button, which turned the screen black. Below the desk, the humming of the hard drive also ended. ". . .What the hell happened?"

Behind them, an old set of *Encyclopedia Britannica* from the top cabinets came crashing down by their feet. They didn't move a muscle.

Mark leaned close to Rachel's ear. "We have entered the *Twilight Zone*."

Rachel patted his chin. "Let's check out their rooms."

He shook his head at Larry. "Private Investigator Rachel Yards."

"Come on, sweetie." Rachel tapped his stomach. "Move back so I can get out."

Stephanie and Larry pointed at the carpet. "What about the books?" The others dragged them out of Reference.

On the third floor of a freshman dorm on the east end of campus, Rachel knocked on the open doorframe. "Hello? Anybody here?"

From the bathroom came voices on a radio—the play-by-play of a Yankees game. A scrawny, bare-chested eighteen-year-old, brushing his teeth, staggered to the door. "Whatta ya want?" His uneven eyebrows rose, and he ran to his messy bed for a shirt and buttoned it unevenly.

"Hello." Rachel waved at him. "I'm Rachel Yards." The others remained outside.

He lowered his head, causing a glob of toothpaste to fall to the carpet, while he considered her legs. He coughed, since he'd almost swallowed his toothpaste in the process. He wiped the foam off his mouth.

Rachel asked, "May we come in?" Opposite her, horizontal bars of light were falling on the floor.

The freshman nodded, noticing a pile of underwear and socks near her feet. "I'm, uh, Ralph Ford." They shook hands. The softness of her fingers, and the aroma of her perfume, made him tingle all over.

Rachel felt Mark slip his arm around her waist. "The hunk with the goatee is Mark Lexington."

"How are you doing?" Mark shook the kid's hand, almost pulling him forward, his broad shoulders too much of a match for Ralph's.

Motioning with her arm, Rachel smiled. "The tall guy is Larry Moore. And that's Stephanie Brooks."

Larry shook the youngster's hand; Stephanie waved from the doorway. The boy's closet door remained partially open, half hiding the unmade bed near an empty desk and bookcase in the far corner.

Waving the toothbrush, Ralph kept staring into Rachel's eyes. "Can you excuse me for a second?"

"Sure. He seems like a nice kid," she whispered to the others. Sarah Appleton's roommate had left for the weekend.

Toothbrush and paste gone except for a smudge on his pointy chin, hair combed sideways, shirt buttoned correctly, he was soon asking, "Aren't you the deejays from the radio station?"

"Yes." Rachel had slipped closer to Ralph when she saw three pictures of blondes in bikinis between the windows. She smoothed out his collar. "I heard Melvin enjoyed my show."

"Ha?" Ralph shook his head. At five-seven, he was eye-level with her, but he couldn't resist glancing for a moment at her boobs. "No. Mel loved food."

Everyone burst out laughing.

Rachel asked, "What else did he like?"

He placed his hands on his longer-than-average-neck. "He kept talking about multiculturalism and eastern philosophy. Didn't like Freud and Darwin, big names on this campus. Since the world is too complex to survive, Melvin said you need a more diverse curriculum to learn everything. Complained about the reading selections. Too much Western thought."

Rachel turned with raised eyebrows to Mark, who shrugged. "What else?"

Ralph lowered his arms. "He was always talking about civil rights, animal rights, equal rights for women. Global warming." He rubbed the stubble at his cheekbone with the side of his thumb. "Remember last month when the NRA had their convention nearby, and there was that small protest on campus? He was one of the organizers. He said the founding fathers were racists, adulterers, and killers of Indians."

Larry said, "Sounds like you didn't share your roommate's beliefs."

Ralph crossed his arms. "He was too much of a radical to live with. And he was always eating, up to midnight. I'm sorry he's gone. His parents were here yesterday, demanding some kind of action. But since the killer's been caught. . . ."

Stephanie wedged herself between them. "When was the last time you saw Melvin?"

"Like I told the police and the men from the prosecutor's office, he and his people had a meeting at Memorial Hall at 9:30 Thursday night."

The four seniors looked at each other. It was a quarter mile east of Knights Hall.

Ralph tapped Rachel's shoulder. "How. . .uh, how'd you know Melvin lived here?"

"We asked downstairs." Rachel gave him a hug, much to his surprise. "Thank you for your help."

Outside in the sunlight, strolling past a show of flowers on a grass-bordered path between the gray-stone freshman dorm and Knights Hall, Stephanie pointed to a concrete bench. "Oh, my God. That wasn't there earlier." On the bench, a white mask was resting on a sealed envelope.

Rachel picked up the mask and put it on her face. "What do you think?"

The others shook their heads.

She ripped open the envelope. *To: Rachel Yards*, it read, and contained a brief note: *You're skating on thin ice.  When it cracks and plunges you into the cold water, no one will be around to hear you scream or to lend a hand.*

Crumpling the note, she smiled.  "We're on the right track."

# CHAPTER 6

HOURS AFTER EATING their Sunday dinner and playing cards in the Marshall Complex, the four were laughing on their way back to the dorms. Under a cloudy, moonless sky, Rachel remarked, "Isn't that a gargoyle above the door of Temple Hall? I just realized that." The gray gothic building west of Davis Hall rose five stories to a peaked roof. Ivy surrounded the square windows. Beside the bronze doors, two hungry lions sat on all fours. "I've been in there once or twice." She studied the door. The constant movement of branches was breaking up the light from lamp and telephone poles.

Stephanie brought her glasses further up the bridge of her nose. "A larger version of the one in the old library."

Before the guys could say anything, the girls pulled them toward the building.

Except for music in the distance, the alley remained quiet.

Larry pointed. "The lights are on. Who'd be working there now?"

Rachel raised her eyebrows. "We'll soon find out."

A squirrel cut across their path and dashed up a tree.

Mark turned the brass knob. "It's unlocked." Rachel pushed him forward. He held back. "Hold your horses, sweetheart."

"No time." Her shoes soon clicked down the marble hallway. "Nice furniture." Antique chairs and tables sat along the white stucco walls. On a door three paces in, a sign read *Conference Room.*

Looking through a glass-paneled classroom door, Stephanie shivered and rubbed her arms. "Not only are the lights on, but *again* with the air conditioner."

Mark ran past Stephanie, and the door to the History Department, to catch up to Rachel. "Hey, careful. We don't want to run into any robed guys."

Larry pointed above them. "Check out the chandelier."

Stephanie stared at it, too—apple-shaped, suited more for a ballroom than a college building. Large portraits of the founding fathers hung on the walls. "Oh, my *God.*"

Larry sprinted to Stephanie to catch her before she fell to the floor. "She's fainted." He felt her pulse. "She's okay." He began tapping her cheek. "Wake up, Steph. Wake up."

Mark asked, "What the hell. . . ?"

Rachel whistled. "Cool."

Five feet off the floor, the ghost of a legless man, reading a book, hovered in front of a portrait of George Washington issuing orders to his troops.

Eyebrows raised, Mark murmured, "My brother told me about ghosts roaming Davis Hall. I didn't know about this building."

Rachel smiled. "We should talk to him. . . . *It.*"

Mark shook his head. "Remember the beginning of *Ghost-*

*busters*, when they were at the public library and saw that ghost hanging in the air? When the guys said, 'Get her,' it sprang at them with long arms and a mouth full of fangs!"

"That's the *movies*." Two steps closer to the ghost, she knocked on the armrest of a couch. "Excuse me, Mr. Spirit."

The ghost turned its head toward them.

Mark spun her around by her shoulder. "I'm serious. It's not a good idea to disturb a spirit in this dimension."

"Let go of me! I want to talk to him."

"It's dangerous to mess with the unknown, Rach!"

Stephanie mumbled, "They're arguing over a ghost!"

Larry motioned to Steph to look up.

Mark whispered, "Who do you think he is?"

"A former professor," said Rachel, "who knows about the robed guys."

Smiling, the ghost nodded and flew down the hallway, past the remaining portraits, and out of the building between an exit sign and a clock above the rear door.

Rachel sank into Mark's grip. "Did he hear me?"

Larry caught Stephanie before she almost fainted again.

"What's this?" Rachel scampered to the couch. She bent over to pick up a book the size of a photo album. "It's a—a *diary* of sorts. Maybe a journal." She started flipping the pages.

Heart beating like mad, Mark came up alongside her. "What did you find?"

"A notebook. . .on the history of the university."

Larry and Stephanie joined them. "A clue about the secret society, Rachel?"

Rachel frowned. "Stephanie, you're so pale."

"No shit!"

The slamming of the conference room door made them turn their backs to the portraits. Rachel raised her eyebrows. "Dean Sands!"

"What are you four doing in here?" asked the tall man with the rectangular face.

"We saw a ghost." Rachel hid the book behind her back.

The others stared at her.

"*Ghost?*" The dean raised an eyebrow. "You need psychological help, my dear." The muscles on his wrinkled face and neck tightened. "What's that behind your back, Rachel?"

Rachel ran her tongue over her teeth. "Search me."

"Professor Wells tells me, Miss Yards," the Dean said with a frown, "that lately you've been interested in secret societies. Odd for a disc jockey."

Rachel smiled. "When I came across—"

Mark bumped her shoulder.

"Are you keeping tabs on me?"

"Listen, young lady." His lips twisted and his brown eyes grew darker. "Sometimes what you don't know won't hurt you, but if you keep digging—" he moved toward Rachel but grabbed Stephanie's wrist.

"Hey, let go of me!" the blonde demanded.

Larry snapped, "You can get arrested for assaulting a student."

Stopping in his tracks, Sands snarled, "I'm the dean of this university. Whose word would the administration believe? Mine, or that of a bunch of troublemakers who see ghosts? Put *that* in the school newspaper!" He led Stephanie to the back door, followed by the others. "Now, go back to your dorms."

Once they heard the door lock behind them, Larry asked, "Stephanie, you all right?"

She shook her arm. "Yes. Thanks."

Glaring at Rachel, Mark asked, "Why did you say we saw a ghost?"

Cradling the book in her arms, she said, "I figured maybe he'd leave us alone if he thought we're crazy."

Later, sitting on the edge of Mark's bed in the men's dorm, Rachel had her legs crossed and was paging through the brown diary in the light of a goose lamp at the foot of the desk. "Did you know women weren't admitted into this university until 1975?"

"So?" Mark replied. "West Point didn't allow 'em until 1976."

"You're right," Rachel grumbled. "Hey, would you believe that, in 1901, the first incoming class consisted of only twenty students?"

Sitting next to her, Stephanie yawned. "Place sure has grown."

Rachel turned a page. "'We have produced lawyers, doctors, dentists, CEOs, government officials, judges, prosecutors, and we've sent men to the moon.'"

Rubbing his bare feet along Rachel's back, Mark asked, "Astronauts have come here?"

Rachel shrugged. "There's more. 'A student body that already has a socio-economic advantage will be easier to teach the fundamentals of Western thought than those who don't. This will provide for a brighter future for America!'"

Lightning flashed. "It says here, 'Knights Hall is the oldest building on campus, built in the eye of the hurricane, with tentacles that reach further out than the White House.'"

"Eye of the hurricane?"

"Tentacles that—"

"Tunnels?"

A clap of thunder drowned their voices.

Rachel had turned the book ninety degrees to look at a map. "The school was originally laid out like a pyramid."

"Eye of the hurricane." Mark ran his fingers over his goatee. "The all-seeing eye of the pyramid."

Rachel flipped pages. "The guy's name was Leonard Schmidt. He was a professor at Harvard who resigned because of an attempted lynching. He believed language, communication, and philosophy were the greatest achievements of man. Adored monks because of their quest for knowledge. And was intrigued by knights, because they were both warriors and protectors." She snapped the book shut with a thud and jumped off the bed. "When we return to Knights Hall, we have to find those tunnels. Like the one we ran through when we escaped." She began to pace the length of the bed. "We also need to find blueprints of this campus. They're probably in President O'Connor's office."

Stephanie looked at her fingernails. "Knights. Warriors. It's ironic how this dorm is called Swords Hall."

"We should check out this building for tunnels, too." Rachel bent down to pick up an undershirt and tossed it onto a chair. "Somehow, we also have to get into the clock tower."

Rain began to spatter the windows.

"Wait," said Stephanie. "You're talking about trespassing. Breaking and entry. . . ."

"Relax, silly." Rachel tapped her friend's knee with the diary and sat down. "What else can we find?"

The guys lowered their heads.

Stephanie frowned. "Why are you, like, a female Indiana

Jones?"

Searching the pages, Rachel smiled. "When my family went camping in upstate New York, my brothers and I used to explore caves, sometimes at night. Not far from my house in Toms River, we checked out the haunted houses in Mantoloking, too, along the shore in the evening. We'd walk under the rides at Seaside Heights and get splashed by the ocean in the winter. We'd hang out under the boardwalk to tell ghost stories. So, yeah."

Mark asked, "Did you practice any dark magic?"

Rachel shook her head. "It says here, 'This school has been plagued by too many disappearances. The executions must stop!'" A rumble of thunder made her jump. ". . .*This* is interesting. 'In the past thirty years, events here at the university have grown tougher to *control*, with the push for faith, Eastern philosophy pouring in like a flood, the avalanche of multiculturalism, political correctness, the addition of others, and, although they are an art form, the distractions of women.'" Rachel laid the diary on Mark's dusty dresser. "His last entry was February 2000." She nodded, her expression grave, and looked out the window. The rain continued to beat on the glass. Her round nose touched the cold surface, and she froze.

Three floors below, in the storm, five robed men with white masks were raising swords above their heads on the grass.

"My God!" Rachel dropped to her knees. "They're after us."

"Rachel!"

"Who's there?"

Mark lifted her to her feet, bumping the lamp. "What did you see?"

She told him.

Larry looked out the window, with Stephanie leaning on his back. "I don't see anyone."

"Same here."

A flash of lightning pushed them away from the window.

After a deep breath, Rachel cried, "We have to hide the diary."

Silence descended.

The guys looked at each other. "We'll keep it." It was Mark speaking. "We can hide it in a good spot."

"Good," Rachel said. "I'm ready to take on those guys."

"Listen, Miss America." Mark had blocked her path. "The two of you should stay here. If you want, we can escort you to your dorms. But make sure you lock your doors."

Stephanie crossed her arms. "I vote for staying here."

Rachel hugged him. "An escort would be great."

Fifteen minutes later, the girls were sleeping, but Rachel was having nightmares about monks chasing them across the campus.

# CHAPTER 7

ONDAY MORNING, THERE WERE blue skies south of the softball field. Rachel and the others were strolling to class with the girls in front when a freshman named Ralph Ford approached them to ask, "Hey, what's up?"

Rachel smiled. "Hi, Ralph."

"Sarah Appleton's roommate, Barbara Quorke, wants to talk to you guys," replied the scrawny boy with a long neck. "She's by the entrance of the tennis courts. You can't miss her. She's the pretty redhead."

Rachel kissed him on the nose. "That's great, Ralph."

Barbara, who had been keeping an eye on her watch, looked up to find them from where she was standing in front of sticker bushes and a green fence behind which two male professors were playing tennis. "Rachel Yards?"

"Yes." They shook hands.

The slender, well-endowed girl, who was still wearing braces, put her books down on the sidewalk. "Ralph told me about your visit to his dorm. When I heard Melvin disappeared, it reminded me of Sarah, because the two of them helped organize the NRA protest, you know. . . . It scared me. . .too coincidental."

Rachel stepped over a small puddle. "Anything you can tell us about her?"

The freshman's auburn eyebrows rose. "She was a feminist, for one. Always pushing for women's studies. Last time anybody ever saw her was at an Order of Women meeting at Welch Hall. At the end of it, she got a phone call from a friend off campus. She was never seen again. I. . .I put out my own missing person flyers." She sniffled. "Her parents were heartbroken when they heard she was missing. But at least they caught that killer! Maybe it'll bring the poor people some closure. . . . I was questioned by campus security and the police."

Stephanie cleared her throat. "Did the police, Sergeant Dolan, ever discover who called Sarah?"

Barbara shook her head.

"I came across a Professor Welch, also from Harvard, in the diary," said Rachel, more to her friends than to the eighteen-year-old.

Sneakers continued to squeak on the court nearest them as the two players exchanged volleys.

Barbara's eyes grew moist. "I liked Sarah, but she was weird. She wouldn't let her picture get taken, 'cause she thought her soul would go to hell. She'd put up her arms and shout, 'No. No. No!' when someone held a camera at her."

Mark pressed his lips together. "Did she do or say anything else odd?"

Barbara thought about it. "For Christmas break, a bunch of us flew to Florida. Sarah didn't go swimming. She knows how, but she didn't own a bathing suit. We offered ours. . . . How could someone go to Daytona without a bathing suit?"

"Maybe," Stephanie suggested, "she almost drowned when she was young or something."

The redhead shrugged. "She never said anything."

Larry asked, "What kind of stuff did she read?"

Another shrug. "Stuff from NOW and other feminist groups."

Larry turned to Mark. "I remember her name, and Melvin's, from when we wrote that article about the protest for the paper."

Two birds flew past them overhead. Barbara said, "I almost forgot, Sarah dumped a guy because his parents were divorced. She had said, 'Marriage is forever.'"

The seniors were speechless. An airplane roared by on its way to Canada.

Rachel pointed. "I love that skirt."

The freshman smiled. "I bought it at Bloomingdale's. Too bad, but Sarah couldn't afford anything like this because the private school had drained her parents of thousands of dollars. That's why she qualified for tons of financial aid. And she never wear shorts, but she always had tight jeans."

From among a crowd of students passing between the tennis courts and a gray building, Professor Wells called out, "Stop bothering that young lady and get to class," before marching off.

Before Rachel could speak, Stephanie and Mark pushed her.

Eyes still filled with dismay, Quorke mumbled, "I'd better go. Been nice talking to you. You know where to find me." She picked up her books and headed south.

"Damn you two." Rachel almost dropped her own books. "Did ya see that?"

Stephanie took a step next to her friend. "You saw them, too?"

". . .See what?" Mark asked.

Rachel pointed at a senior dorm opposite the tennis courts. "Two men wearing white masks on the roof of the building. Last week's party at Marsh?"

Mark turned to the girls. "In broad daylight? . . . Either these people are getting desperate, or they're really pissed off."

Larry said, "Let's drop this."

"*No!*" Rachel stomped her foot. "Melvin and Sarah protested against the NRA. They had radical views, and they both disappeared. Something is *happening* on this campus."

Stephanie kicked a rock into the puddle. "Rachel, lower your voice."

Rachel grumbled, "The answer's in that diary."

Grabbing hold of Rachel's shoulders, Mark said, "Okay, calm down. We'll see this through. It's just I don't want to see anybody get hurt."

She kissed his goatee. "Believe me, we won't." They left.

The two middle-aged professors, one with a mustache, one without, towels around their necks, bottles of water and rackets in their hands, had been standing by the net since Wells came and went. The taller of the two put down his racket to punch a pre-recorded number into his cell phone.

By afternoon, the sunshine held, abetted by white clouds; as she was descending the steps of Knights Hall after a 1:00 PM class, Rachel's cell rang. "Hello, Mark. What's up? . . . Okay. Catch ya later, sweetie. . . . The guys want to meet us at Freemun's Pond in two hours."

Stephanie was surprised. "They say why?"

"No."

Two classes later, they were sitting on a park bench with their legs crossed, backs to the stone building, facing the pond where a school of ducks was competing for pieces of bread that had been thrown into the water by another student despite the warning signs. "From when I was a kid until I started attending college—" Rachel scratched her bare knee, then tossed her blue skirt hem over it— "we used to go crabbing at the bay near Seaside Heights. We'd be there for *hours*. Three times we got caught in a storm, but we crabbed anyway."

Stephanie frowned. "That explains it. Your whole family is crazy. My sister and I played with doll houses."

Rachel smiled when the guys arrived, wearing sunglasses. "What's so important we had to meet here for you to tell us?"

Mark studied her. "Don't get upset, but the diary's gone."

"*What?*" Both girls uncrossed their legs and moved to the edge of the bench.

"Calm down," Larry demanded, sitting on the other bench. "There was also a note. It read, *Now you see it, now you don't.*"

Though Stephanie sank into the bench, Rachel leaped for Mark, who was standing at the edge of the pond. "The diary's gone?"

He side-armed a stone into the water. "It scares the shit out of me, and it pisses me off to think someone was in our room."

"When did this *happen?*" Rachel reached for him, but he stepped sideways.

"After we left the room, and before I called you."

Stephanie said, "Should we go to campus security?"

"Steph." Larry had reached for her shoulder. "We got the diary from a ghost. How credible is that?"

Stephanie squeezed his hand. "I'll call Sergeant Dolan."

Mark turned to take a drink at the water fountain next to the benches.

Tapping her heels on the black walkway, Rachel announced, "We should search for that diary, and I bet you Professor Wells' office is a great place to start."

Mark seized her arms, forcing her backward and scaring a squirrel into the grass. "It's *over!* Those monks have the ability to go anywhere they want or do anything they want. They could be watching us right now from any of those windows." Academic and administrative buildings surrounded the pond. Three dorms occupied the southern boundary. "I just want to graduate next month, get my masters, and work at a radio station with the three of you. Understood?"

Rachel burst into tears, laying her head on Mark's chest.

"Oh, God." He hugged her. "Shh. Quiet. I'm sorry." He lifted her head up. "Does it mean that much to you?"

She wiped away her tears. "Yes! Because they might come after us after we graduate."

Larry cleared his throat. "She's got a point. We know quite a bit."

Mark shook his head and sighed, "What do you want to do?"

She returned to the bench. "Have Barbara Quorke or Ralph get Wells out of his office, so we can take a look around."

Stephanie stared at her. "Why involve the freshmen?"

"They seem eager to help, especially Ralph."

Stephanie mumbled, "I'll be the fool to ask. Rachel, when do you want to do this?"

"Tonight!"

# CHAPTER 8

PEN IN HAND, PROFESSOR WELLS looked up from his desk when a young man came running in, almost knocking over a chair, screaming about someone needing help. "Calm *down*, son!" He leaned forward. "Take a deep breath."

The boy did.

Wells tossed his pen on the paper he was grading. "Now, what's wrong?"

"I'm, uh, Ralph Ford," said the freshman in a shaky voice. "My friend Barbara Quorke is. . . . Oh, *hurry*." He grabbed the man's hand and pulled him out of the room, leaving the light on.

Two minutes later, Rachel led her crew into the office. Rounding the desk, she ordered, "Stephanie, check out the computer. Mark, go through the file cabinets. And Larry, look for safes behind the pictures. I'll search the desk."

Stephanie pulled the armchair to the computer.

Opening a drawer, Mark asked, "What are we looking for?"

Rachel was flipping through the pages under Wells' pen. "Anything about monks or disappearances." She shifted another pile of papers by the corner but found nothing to her liking. When she opened a Western literature text, the telephone rang, which made her jump, and everyone else froze. After a fourth ring, she saw no flashing on the other key pads. "Nothing. Person hung up, thank God." She opened the top left drawer.

Stephanie whispered, "What's that smell?"

Next to framed pictures of Wells' family, Rachel noticed an ashtray. "He smokes cigars." In the center drawer, she found office supplies. "Everything is so organized and dust-free, it's disgusting."

"Damn," Mark muttered. One of the drawers wouldn't open. "Locked."

Larry cleared his throat. "There's a safe here behind the picture of John Harvard."

Rachel, who had been searching through the bottom drawer, asked, "Steph, you find anything yet?"

Behind her near a bookcase, the blonde was staring at the screen. "It says here, 'Books on Zen and Buddhism have been returned, but the school received double the order of books on Plato, Socrates, and Aristotle.'"

"So?" Rachel stood up with a notebook she'd found.

Stephanie closed that file and clicked on another icon. "From what Ralph and Barbara said, and what was written in the diary, Eastern philosophy is a crime at this school. Besides, Wells's the English department chair. Why should he care about philosophy books?"

Rachel opened his appointment book. "You got a point."

"Hey, Rach." Stephanie adjusted her glasses. "Look at this!"

"What?"

Stephanie scrolled down the screen. "Info about the ghost we saw in Temple Hall."

"You're kidding." Rachel turned around. "How did you find it?"

Stephanie smiled. "I clicked on a Knight icon, typed in 'Yale' as a password, and *voila*."

Rachel hit the chair. "Way to go, girl!"

Stephanie read aloud, "'Leonard Schmidt was expelled from Harvard for threatening to compromise a student aide because the student-teacher was anti-evolution. Blah blah blah. . . . He started here in 1990. He became a Knight in 1991. He taught philosophy. Blah blah. . . . He died choking on food.'" The girls stared at each other.

Mark slammed a drawer.

Larry came over to him. "That's it for the pictures. The portraits of Reagan and Washington didn't budge. Wells was a lineman at Yale."

Stephanie read on. "'He believed in the Knight's philosophy and goals of capitalism, secularism, Western thought, the dominance of white males, the right to bear arms, the death penalty, and the separation of church and state, but he also thought the rituals were getting out of hand. The burning of that black kid was too much for him. His soul is trapped forever in this world.'"

Bumping into the desk, Rachel asked her, "Can you print that?"

Stephanie turned on the printer.

Mark asked, "Rach? What's wrong?"

Rachel smiled. "Wells and O'Connor are supposed to have a meeting about me later tonight. Meeting with T. A. What's T. A?"

On his knees, Larry asked, "Mark, can you help me with this one? It's jammed."

Stephanie's voice rose. "They retrieved the diary."

Flipping through the spiral notebook, Rachel mumbled, "No shit."

"Hey, Rach," Stephanie gasped, "I think you better have a look at this."

Rachel sighed. "That's a horrible picture of me."

"Your bio is listed: dark hair, five-seven, Communications major, deejay, former athlete. . . . You're on their files as a danger-ous troublemaker who should be closely watched, and all you can say is *that?*" Stephanie clicked that file closed. "These perverts have your *measurements.*"

Rachel shrugged, holding onto the book and continuing to search the desk.

"Yes," Mark said. "Look at this." He pulled out an old map of the campus.

"Excellent, sweetie."

They heard three loud sneezes in rapid session from the hallway. The four stared at each other. "The closet!" Rachel motioned to the door in the near corner. "Steph, return to the original. . . ."

Stephanie mumbled, "I know what to do."

After the guys stuffed the map back inside, they began shaking the drawer. "It won't shut."

Rachel shoved the chair up, rattling the items on the desk. "Guys. . . . Quiet."

"Finally." They ran to the closet and had eased the door closed a moment before Wells reentered his office. In the gloom, the other three pointed at Rachel, who had the professor's book in her hands. She cringed.

Two steps inside the room, Wells stopped to stare at the pictures of Eisenhower, Lincoln, and Rockefeller. Grumbling under his breath, he straightened them. As he neared his desk, he noticed the green printer light was on. "I thought I turned that off." He bent down to touch the button. When he stood up, he saw his nameplate had been moved to the edge of his desk. He huffed, "What's going on here?"

Rachel's eyes widened when she saw a white mask and brown robe lying on a suitcase on a shelf in the closet. A sword resting in its scabbard sat next to the outfit. Opposite her, between Mark and Larry, Stephanie muffled a sneeze the best she could.

Wells turned toward the closet, blocking the light under the door.

When Wells' hand was inches from the doorknob, the phone rang. "Who could that be?" He turned back to the telephone. "Wells."

The kids took a long, deep breath.

"What? . . . *What* happened to my car?" He shoved the chair against the desk. "A senior tried to avoid a pot hole in the wrong lot and hit my *brake light?*" He pounded a pile of papers. "I'll be right there." He slammed the receiver. "What a night." He pulled down the shades, found his briefcase, swung around the desk for the jacket hanging behind the door, switched off the light, and locked the door.

Rachel stuck her head out the closet door. "He's gone."

Larry pushed the door further open. "That was too close. My heart was pounding."

"Mine, too." Once Stephanie's eyes adjusted to the darkness, she asked, "What were you motioning toward in the closet?"

Mark examined the door. "It's locked from the outside. Now

what?"

Filing Wells' appointment book in the desk drawer, Rachel said, "We'll climb out the window."

"What?"

Rachel smiled. "Why not? We're on the second floor. What's the big deal? The closet. . .I saw Wells' robe, mask, and sword inside."

The others sighed.

"Come *on*." Rachel clapped. "Just don't stand there! We gotta go!"

Ready to climb over the desk, Stephanie pointed at Rachel. "You first."

Once they were on the grass, Rachel broke off a twig from a nearby bush below the windows the four had used a thick pipe to climb down from, and said, "Now, that's what I call exciting."

"Exciting?" Stephanie exclaimed. "I call it crazy."

Rachel pressed a finger to her lips. "Let's go to the dorms to check out what you got off the computer."

"Good idea," Mark said. "I'll diagram the map for you." They left under a pitch-black sky, a whipping wind. . .and the eyes of the monks.

ON TUESDAY MORNING, Rachel was standing at the doorway to Loyal Hall, southwest of Nicky's Field, another gothic building distinguished by columns and archways. She put on her sunglasses and said, "We have about ten minutes before class starts, so relax."

Larry was reading his textbook for an upcoming exam in communications. None of them had studied for it.

Stephanie coughed. "Rach, you have an idea? What is it?"

Rachel gestured. "Look around. The student body is composed of mostly white guys and girls who are rich, socially well-to-do, in good shape, and clean-cut. They're all of a certain mold."

Above her, against the railing, Mark chuckled. "See the tall kid there smoking a cigarette, with the long hair and the KISS Tee shirt? He's atypical." He snapped his fingers. "Wait a minute—KISS stands for Knights In Satan's Squadron."

"Ha! So."

An increase in student traffic going in and out of the building silenced the discussion.

Mark lifted his sunglasses to wipe his eyes. "In Mr. Loom's accounting class, I saw another kid with the Federal Reserve book, *Secrets of the Temple*. K & T. Knights Hall and Temple Hall. They consider Knights University a temple, and they protect it like they're knights."

Stephanie's eyebrows rose. "Sounds like a fascist plot."

From the top step, Larry said, "I've heard from the other reporters that the students here come mostly from private schools or top public schools. No radical. . . ."

Dean Sands was approaching the building from Freemum Hall. "Well, well. If it isn't the ghost chasers!" He paused at the steps, briefcase dangling at his knees. "Just because your last semester is ending, that doesn't give you the right to dawdle before class. But since I have your attention, four students were seen climbing down Temple Hall near Dr. Wells' office last night. Couldn't've been you, could it?" He stared at Rachel. The kids called him Frankenstein because of the angular shape of his head and his wide, flat nose.

Rachel laid a hand on her throat. "A frail young thing like me?"

The dean leaned closer. "You're not so frail, darling. You

played soccer and basketball this year. How come you're not playing softball?"

Rachel tucked strands of hair behind her ear. "It's more exciting
to chase ghosts and find buried treasure."

"You keep that up, and you'll go to the funny-farm penniless."
Dean Sands looked at her in utter disdain, climbed a step, and
turned to Larry and Stephanie. "Wells had a rough night. He took
care of a sick freshman. His car was hit by an intoxicated student
in the teacher's parking lot. And a bunch of gremlins messed with
his desk and computer."

The sun had disappeared behind the clouds.

Larry's Adam's apple rippled. "What do you mean?"

Before Sands could respond, Stephanie asked, "Do you keep
tabs on Professor Wells?"

Sands clenched his teeth, and lines emerged on his high forehead. "He told the administration what happened. He had to fill
out an accident and health report, my dear."

Rachel asked, "Sir, where did you go after you saw us in Temple
Hall Sunday night?"

". . .What business is it of yours?"

Rachel's hand curled against the soft curve of the moleskin skirt
she was wearing with a white silk blouse. "Put on your monk's uniform, did you, along with your buddies, bring swords, to try and
scare us in the rain?"

The others had grown pale.

Sands smiled. "Rachel, I haven't dressed up for Halloween and
gone trick-or-treating since I was a kid."

"You think that was a joke?"

Sands shook his briefcase against his leg. "Joke? No. This isn't a freak show either. It's one of the best universities in the country. It has the finest reputation, sits on a gorgeous campus in the mountains—you're not going to change that. I've been here for thirty-five years, and. . .and I don't plan on retiring any time soon."

She moisten her upper lip with her tongue. "Who *were* the monks with the swords?"

He stepped back. "Probably your ghost and his buddies from Temple Hall."

She kept staring at the man. "Who was *he*? How did he become a spirit?"

He coughed. "You mean to tell me you didn't get his story yourself, Rachel? You're slipping."

She took a step forward. "I figure a man of your stature would know everything about this place."

"I know what's real and what's not. Ghosts fall into the category of make-believe."

"Western philosophy is also made-up stuff." She smiled, noticing the frown forming around his mouth and a darkness entering his eyes. "Old men spitting out catch phrases about life like advertisers peddling a product."

By then, he was frowning. "Excuse me!" He took a deep breath. "Western philosophy is a set of guidelines that motivates people to behave properly, that offers them reasonable explanations of life. It teaches critical thinking and logical analysis. An example of that was The Enlightenment, brought to the colonies by Thomas Jefferson and Benjamin Franklin. Philosophy is based in *reason*. It is the attempt to understand who we are and what we think of ourselves. That in turn allows us to develop ideas about reality, ethics, knowledge, politics, religion, and art. Philosophy is not an abstract subject to be ridiculed. On the other hand, these ghosts you're seeing are probably horrible memories from a childhood full of struggle, difficulty, and violence."

Her smile faded. "I had a very good childhood. Very peaceful. Though, yes, we did tell stories about haunted houses and Jersey Ghosts."

"Precisely what I mean. Those activities generated such fear in you, you believe you're seeing spirits and monks carrying swords."

She stepped back to the railing. Sunlight had again been shining on her for some time. The others remained speechless. Smile forming on her face, renewed strength in her voice, she said, "I'm afraid of capitalism, not ghosts."

"That's very odd." He scratched his eyebrow. "Capitalism is what drives this country."

"It suppresses people."

He checked his watch. "It gives them jobs, a feeling of accomplishment, liberates their ideas, and produces goods and services."

She noticed the edge of a tattoo beneath his watch. "Capitalism has made this place pretty expensive."

Turning to the doorway, he said, "Judging from your outfit, you have nothing to worry about."

She squared her shoulders. "Is that social sarcasm?"

He shook his head. "It's a compliment. If you'll forgive me, I have business here. Good day." He entered the building.

Stephanie asked Rachel, "What were you doing?"

Rachel smiled. "Trying to break him. I did make him nervous."

Reaching for Rachel's hand, Mark said, "We'd better get inside."

# CHAPTER 9

STANDING IN HEELS AT THE EDGE of a wet towel on the tile floor of their bathroom, Stephanie shouted over the Pearl Jam CD from the ledge above the toilet and the running water of the shower, "Rachel! *Rachel*!"

Rachel slid back the floral plastic curtain a few inches. "What's up?"

"Larry and I," Stephanie shouted, "are going to Shields Bar to see the Battle of the Bands. It starts at eight. Will you and Mark be joining us later?" She couldn't even see herself in the steam-covered mirror. The water vapor hanging in the air gave her bare legs a chill.

"You bet! Station's sponsoring it." Rachel wiped water off her face. "Sorry. I'm running late. Professor Drake kept Mark and me in Philo. He'll be here soon."

"Great." Stephanie smiled. "Oh, Rach. Please be careful with the toilet. It's acting up again." A puddle surrounded it and lined the shower. "That's why the plunger's there." She pointed to her left. A brown towel and a green robe were lying on the toilet seat.

"Got it." Rachel shut the curtain.

"I'll leave your desk lamp on." Hurrying out, Stephanie said to Larry, who was waiting by the door near the closets, "They'll meet us. She's sorry for running late." She switched off the main light. "Bye!" She called out. They shut the door.

After Rachel finished shampooing her hair, she turned off the water by yanking the handles tight because of an occasional drip. Once she tied the strap of her robe, she pushed open the curtains, jiggling the rings on the horizontal bar, and stepped onto the wet towel. In one class, she'd shown up in a bathrobe but been asked to change by the professor. She wrapped the towel around her hair. She thought she heard a noise—all four had keys to each other's rooms. "...Mark. Is that you? Stephanie? Larry? Did ya forget something?" The only other voice in the room was Eddie Vader singing about Jeremy's strange laughter. She figured she was hearing things and wiped the middle of the mirror with the palm of her hand. Whistling to the song, she looked down at the cluttered counter for a tube of face cream, but when she lifted her head back up, she froze. The tube remained in her grip. Slowly, she lowered it to the counter and walked her fingers to two cans closer to the medicine cabinet. She began to shake.

There was a squish, and the two monks looked at each other. The tall one's work boot had touched the wet towel. They leaped for the girl.

She spun around, spraying the cans of hair spray at them as she screamed for her life.

The two began to shout and rub their eyes.

She threw the cans at them and reached for the plunger, swung it at them like a baseball bat, slugging both in the stomach. As she shoved her way past them, the short monk pulled the towel off her head. She screamed so loud, they flinched.

She noticed they had killed the light and shoved a desk chair underneath the door knob. Dropping the plunger, she grabbed the front of the seat, heaved the chair at them, and bolted into the hallway, almost knocking over Mark. "Thank God you're here!"

"Rachel! What the hell?" His mouth opened wide when the two shouting monks, stumbling and bumping into each other, came out after her. "You *bastards!*" He pulled Rachel behind him as the intruders barreled past.

A bunch of girls had gathered in the hallway outside their doors. One demanded, "Who the hell are *they?*"

The monks ran up the nearby stairs.

"Let 'em go!" Rachel screamed.

Gripping her shoulders, Mark snarled, "This has gone far enough!"

IN PRESIDENT O'CONNOR'S OFFICE in Temple Hall, Mark and Rachel were holding hands, listening to the hunched-over man as he paced back and forth behind his desk. "Young lady, you don't know the half of it. . . ."

The telephone rang.

O'Connor, trim, with a square head devoid of facial hair, grabbed the receiver, barked, "No calls!" and hung up. He pointed at them. "Miss Yards. Mr. Lexington. You are in way over your heads. I am warning you to drop this matter immediately! If you don't, I will not be able to help you."

When Rachel opened her mouth, Mark squeezed her hand.

"You two," the president went on, "should be concentrating on senior week. Graduation. Grad school. Jobs at a radio station. Marriage."

They blushed.

There was a knock at the door.

"Not *now!*" he shouted without much effort for a seventy-year-old.

Crossing her legs again, Rachel said, "I was attacked in my own room!"

Gulping air, he snapped, "All the more reason to end this quest."

She suddenly grew very still. "How can you let this continue?"

O'Connor leaned over the desk. "If I didn't, I would become another ghost haunting this campus. And I would make sure I was a *scary* motherfucker, Miss Yards, who would turn your black hair white in an instant!"

A chill raced through her, aided by the sleeveless dress that fell no further than her knees.

He sighed. "Can you imagine the nightmares I've had about what happens here?"

She lowered her shoulders. "Mr. O'Connor. . .there must be something you can do."

He stared morbidly at her. "You're lucky to be alive! You managed to escape. And be thankful you're well known. Otherwise, you would have become another 'missing student,' another 'strange disappearance.'"

Mark moved to the edge of the chair. "That's insane!"

"The federal government would close this place down."

Rachel turned toward the windows; Mark's neck muscles had tightened.

Grinning wanly, the president said, "*Now* do you understand the magnitude of the situation? More goes on here than kidnapping and murder. . . ." He massaged the back of his neck. "This university has become my life. An authentic home for many thousands. I would be lost without it." He sighed. "My lovely wife has been dead for seventeen years. Cancer ate her up." He stared at her picture on the desk. "This keeps me going. I've been dedicated to the administration, the faculty, and the students."

Rachel sat up. "Could have fooled me."

O'Connor muttered, "You don't remotely understand the tightrope I have to walk every day, every working hour, to maintain a balance."

Half out of his seat, Mark barked, "Well, then, we'll go to the state police."

The president sighed again. "With what evidence? A diary from a ghost? Nonsense from a couple of scared freshmen? Printouts from an illegally obtained computer file?"

The two seniors exchanged looks.

O'Connor retrieved his chair. "Besides, if you seek help outside the university, you'll have signed your death warrant. Other forces. . . ." He came around his desk to where Rachel sat. "Miss Yards, I know I don't have to tell you what a group of unscrupulous men would do to a beautiful young woman like you before they killed you."

She covered her knees.

Mark put his arm around her shoulders.

In his chair, O'Connor lifted the glasses from the chain around his neck. "Do I make myself clear?"

"Yes." They nodded as they got up, and left.

Two steps into the hallway, Rachel dropped her head onto

Mark's shoulder.

After a few minutes of thought, O'Connor removed a flashlight from his bottom drawer. His shoes creaked on the plastic mat. He found a thick bio of J. P. Morgan, tossed it to the carpet, and turned a knob at the back of the shelf that moved an entire wall section sideways, revealing a passage that led to a dark flight of stairs. He took a breath and descended.

In a dark chamber in Knights Hall, he slipped through a door with the legend *Special Education.* Once his eyes had adjusted to the semi-darkness, he was able to make out the two racks, three feet in front of him, occupied by the monks who had failed in their of attack on Rachel Yards. They still had on their masks, but their hands were bloody. He shook his head at them. Yellow candles lined the perimeter of the room. On his right, he shone the flashlight on four sets of double chains with wrist blocks at the end, two feet apart, dangling from a steel beam six feet above the bare floor. Behind them, wooden clubs, black metal clubs with a spike-studded ball attached by a short chain, axes, saws, and picks hung on the twelve-foot wall. In the corner stood an empty iron maiden next to a stretcher. Near the back wall, sealed lanterns full of poisonous liquids occupied a shelf. The smell could have made an unsuspecting person gag. In the far corner, three huge pots of oil sat on oversized burners, and a moveable three-foot scaffolding, operated by a pulley secured by more ropes that hung from wooden beams. A thick iron door to the left had a small opening at eye level with three short bars. O'Connor focused the flashlight on the locked door. "Is anyone in there I don't know about?" In front of the jail stood a bucket of water, against which leaned a long two-by-four. Two separate coils of rope, used to secure a victim's legs and upper body, sat above it much like a garden hose.

Whip in hand, the grandmaster emerged from between the iron racks. "The room's empty, but I would *love* to put the Yards girl and her friends in there before we reeducate them."

O'Connor shone the flashlight on the masked man's chest. "I just scared the shit out of her."

The taller man crossed his arms. "She doesn't scare too easily."

"I heard her crying in the hallway." The president had lowered the beam to the floor. "You leave her alone, and she'll stop. Persist in attacking her, and she'll continue to investigate—and get more people involved. It's up to you."

"You're afraid of her."

"So are you." The older man lifted the light to the racks. "You've never had an adversary like this before. I admire her courage, persistence, intelligence—"

"And her tits."

O'Connor frowned. "*These* schmucks were probably looking at her ass instead of paying attention to what they were doing."

The masked man pumped up his shoulders. "They've learned their lesson. As for her. . . ."

"Leave her *alone!* In less than a month, she and her friends will be gone. It's almost graduation, when we get plenty of attention from outsiders. We don't need any more. Besides, these extracurricular activities have gone far enough!"

"Never!" The man cracked the whip to the cement, sending O'Connor backwards. "My mission in life, *our* mission, *your* mission, is to create conservative-thinking, capitalistic-minded, Western-philosophy-driven young adults who will re-develop America the way the Founding Fathers wanted it! The way. . .we must rid this country of liberal-minded idiots who care more about animals and the environment than the social, economic, and political values enshrined in the Constitution!"

O'Connor turned toward the door.

The two monks began to moan.

Snapping the whip, the man snarled, "Rachel Yards will determine her own fate. Yours was decided fifteen years ago, when you slept with that dumb broad from Florida—the photos of which remain in good hands, my friend."

After a deep breath, O'Connor replied, "I'm going to take this matter up with the Brotherhood in New York City."

"They're on my side."

Henry unlocked the door. "You forget one thing."

"What's that?"

"A highly spirited girl from New Jersey will stop this madness if we don't." He slammed the door shut.

# CHAPTER 10

SETTING DOWN HER BELONGINGS on the counter of the circulation desk, Rachel asked the pudgy librarian, "How much do I owe? These two books are a day late." One was entitled *The Knights Templar*, the other *The Spirit of Radio*.

The man was irritated. "You should be more responsible, young lady."

She twisted her mouth. "Excuse me? Who are you to talk to me that way, my father?" She studied his large nose, wide cheekbones, thick chin, high forehead, and dark hair pushed back. "You look like Stalin. Anyone ever tell you that, buddy? Better lose the mustache."

He coughed. "Aren't you the one who performs witchcraft?" He spun the books halfway around to zap the bar codes with a hand-held scanner plugged into a computer. A brown name tag that read *Knight University, George Heglan, Librarian Assistant* was clipped on the pocket of his long-sleeved green shirt. "That'll be two dollars each."

"What?" She dug into her bag. "Sounds pretty expensive for

one day late." As she shook her head, her sunglasses dropped down the bridge of her nose. Sunlight was falling through small glass panels in the round ceiling of the castle-like tower onto the gray carpet. She laid the sunglasses and a ten-dollar bill on the counter, noticing the school emblem, a gold shield shaped like a triangle, on the rear wall. It had the Latin words *Novus Ordo Seculorum* above and below it. She didn't understand them. On each side stood a Roman scholar. In gray, the school's name, *Knights*, sat dead center, surrounded by roses. She gazed up and grabbed the counter as if someone had stabbed her in the back. He asked if she was all right; she continued to study the portrait of knights on horseback in front of Temple Hall. Hand covering her mouth, she turned slowly, eyes riveted at the panels. They reminded her of when her parents had taken her and her brothers to Saint Patrick's Cathedral to see the figures of Jesus Christ and his disciples on the windows. On these, knights and monks were moving toward the pyramid, with the all-seeing eye directly opposite the circulation desk. "Shit!"

The security guard at the front door, students typing at computers, and a sophomore pushing a cart of books all stopped to stare.

"Young lady!" the librarian whispered hotly. "We don't use foul language in the library!"

"Sorry," she replied in a daze.

"Here's your change."

Rachel regained her composure. "I've been meaning to ask you—how does one become a librarian?"

Heglan laid his hand with the money onto the counter and said, "One earns a master's in Library Science."

Rachel asked, "Why haven't you?"

He leaned backward. "I've been busy doing other things, like writing poetry. Do you want to become a librarian?"

Rachel shook her head. "No. I love radio, where thousands of people can hear your voice, and I find secret societies fascinating."

"Studying secret societies is a waste of time!"

She tore the money out of his hand.

"Rachel." Stephanie had come up to her. "What's wrong? I heard you shout." Rachel whispered in her ear, and Stephanie looked around. "Good God. We better tell the guys."

"You're right, but first I have to go to the bathroom."

Stephanie pointed to a stairway near the bronze doors that led to a lower level. "The ones on this floor aren't working. You gotta go downstairs."

"Thanks." Rachel smiled. "You have to go?"

Stephanie motioned the other way. "I ran out here so fast, I forgot half of my things."

Rachel gestured to the African-American security man sitting by the door. "Meet me over there in five."

Stephanie nodded.

Studying the pyramid and the words *Annuit Coepits* above it, Rachel muttered, "Four years, and I just noticed. . . ."

The stocky guard stood up and leaned toward her when she passed him. "Miss? You okay? Sounded like a heavy discussion. Need anything? . . . By the way, what's so fascinating up there?"

She smiled. "Oh, it's nothing. I'm fine. You're so sweet. Thanks." She disappeared down the circular steps.

When she left the women's bathroom, she heard someone whisper her name.

"Hello?"

"*Rachel.*" The voice was louder this time.

"Yes?" She halted at a water fountain, then turned into a brighter room that contained the demonology and speculation sections. She began to rub her arms. "Who's there?"

On both sides of the shelves, the graffiti-marked desks were empty. "*Rachel.*"

"If this is who I think it is, I'm gonna punch you out." She smacked her fist into her palm.

"*Rachel.*"

She was nearing a horizontal window in the ceiling, wider than she was and open a crack. Sandpaper covered the entire pane. In the corner, a fire extinguisher hung on the far wall. Above her, one of the white panels had been removed with a step- ladder, and other construction equipment stood near by. "*Rachel.*" A chain hung across the doorway to the rear stairs.

Suddenly, her bag swinging through the air, she was lifted off her feet and shoved against a side wall. The back of her head banged hard against the plaster. A powerful hand clutching her throat muffled her cry. Moments later, when she tried another scream, the monk pressed a butcher knife below her left eye. Tears wet the blade. Looking around, she realized she must be a foot off the ground. Hazel eyes were staring at her. A mixture of sweat and after-shave exuded from the man. Her face had become as milky white as the mask. She did notice the edge of a tattoo on the guy's wrist. She knew she'd seen it before.

"Rachel Yards." Another monk, shorter, emerged from the shadows. "This time, you won't get away."

She started to squirm, but when she felt the cold blade pressing harder against her cheekbone, she became still.

Upstairs, between the circulation desk and a line of computers, Stephanie kept fidgeting. "Where *is* this girl?"

"Excuse me, miss." The stocky guard in a blue jacket began motioning to her. "You with the glasses. If you're looking for your friend, she hasn't come up the stairs yet, unless she took the back stairway."

"Thanks!"

"Hey, Blondie," the librarian assistant yelled.

"What?"

He held up Rachel's sunglasses. "Your friend forgot these."

Stephanie jogged over to the main desk.

Downstairs, the shorter monk crossed his arms. "Maybe now Rachel, you'll take President O'Connor's warnings to heart."

Rachel gasped.

"We know everything that goes on here. It's our business to, and to make things happen. We've been doing it for a very long time." He got so close to her, she could smell his breath. "From this point on, you and your friends will concentrate on graduation and leave the operation of this school to us."

She didn't say a word.

"Good," he said.

She knew the person was familiar.

Then from a distance, Stephanie called out, "Rachel! Rachel! Where are you?" The voice grew louder and louder.

"Fuck." Uncrossing his arms, he ordered, "Leave her."

The taller guy dropped Rachel, and they ran down the dark hallway.

She braced the impact with her arms. Her screams were cut off the moment she hit the floor. On her hands and knees, she was coughing and crying.

"Rachel!" Stephanie had thrown her arms around her. "It's over. They're gone. Easy does it."

After a few minutes, Rachel hugged her back. "Thank you so much. Thank you."

Stephanie let go. "What happened?"

"I was. . .I was attacked by two monks."

"Unbelievable." Stephanie helped her stand. "You better freshen up in the bathroom."

Rachel nodded. "Is there a rumor going around about me being a witch?"

Stephanie shrugged.


"DAMN IT!" IN THE GUY'S DORM, Mark threw a crumpled shirt onto his desk. "We agreed to O'Connor's demands!"

Larry shouted, "Calm down! It must've been a radical group . . . ."

"I *won't* calm down!" Mark knocked a pile of books to the floor. Never before had his eyes been so threatening.

"Mark!" Rachel shrieked from the bed. "*Please*, sweetie. Larry's right. It must be people O'Connor doesn't have control over—a really tall guy, and someone with horrible breath."

Larry rubbed his wide chin. "My accounting professor, Dr. Loom, is six-foot-five."

Stephanie had her arm around Rachel's shoulders. "Guys. What does *Novus Ordo Seculorum* mean?"

"New World Order."

"Rach," Mark asked, "Where did those monks go when Steph surprised them?"

She shrugged. "I'm not sure. Down that long hallway, but it was too dark to see for certain."

Larry tapped the shade. "Tunnels?"

Mark asked, "When does the library close?"

"Ten P.M."

Mark smiled. "At eleven-thirty, we sneak into the library through the window Rachel noticed was open."

LEGS DANGLING THROUGH the library window, Stephanie twisted and turned her body. "Jesus. My belt is caught!"

While Rachel and Mark were sliding her legs into the dark room, Larry was easing the rest of her through the opening. "There she goes."

Rachel caught her before she touched the floor.

Larry was already in the room, closing the window.

"Okay, Rach." Mark put a hand on her back. "Where did the monks go?" The light was glinting off a fire extinguisher bolted to the wall.

Rachel pointed with the flashlight. "Down there, toward the center of the building."

At a door marked *Basement*, Rachel clicked her tongue against her upper teeth. "Check out the double lock." The other doors led to a hot-water heater and other plumbing and electrical machinery. In no time, she'd jimmied both locks.

Stephanie's mouth fell open. "Where did you learn how to *do* that?"

Descending the steps with Mark in front, Rachel answered, "In those haunted houses in Mantoloking."

When they had reached the basement's concrete floor and their eyes adjusted to the darkness, they spotted four large archways ahead of them, facing east. Four more stood behind them.

"What's that noise?"

They shone their flashlights to the right and saw a rat scamper along the cinderblock to a hole in the back wall.

Stephanie gasped. "Did you see the *size* of that thing?"

Larry nodded. "Larger than a cat."

"Never mind that." Mark sniffed. "What's that smell? Urine? Body odor?"

Rachel shook her head as she ran her flashlight around the room, seeing spider webs, dripping water, and what looked like bloodstains. "This place reminds me of that haunted hotel in Long Branch, off the Parkway."

Mark pointed to the tunnel on the extreme left. "How about we try that one?"

A few paces into it, Stephanie asked, "How deep underground are we?"

"At least fifteen feet," said Mark, "and we're still descending."

Rachel whispered, "Where are we headed?"

"Davis Hall?" Larry speculated. "The dorms?"

"Probably." Tapping the wall, Mark said, "Shit, they built these passageways to last. Cinderblock on each side, plus the ceiling."

"Hey," Rachel exclaimed after they had gone fifty yards, "we've leveled out, and we're veering left."

Stephanie coughed. "At least that awful smell is gone, but it sure is damp in here, and *dark*."

Rachel cleared her throat. "This explains how they get from one place to another without being spotted. Creepy to think that, while we're asleep, activity goes on here, huh. And it's been happening for a hundred years. Fugitives have probably hidden down these passages."

"Rachel!" Stephanie groaned.

"Now where?" Mark's flashlight had revealed five different pathways. "This's more elaborate than the New York subway system."

Rachel pointed. "Let's try the one in the middle?"

Mark, leading the way, whispered, "In order to build these things, they needed solid ground. That's probably why they chose this terrain."

Rachel agreed. "They'd have a tough time in the Jersey marshes."

Mark pointed. "Up ahead there—I can see wide steps with a railing."

Thirty paces later, they had gathered around the stairs at the end of the tunnel. They climbed them and, at the top, found an iron door.

Rachel reached for the vertical latch. "Where do you think it goes?"

"I. . .I don't believe it," said Mark. They followed him into a cold room.

"We're. . . ." Stephanie's teeth were chattering. "That's a coffin. We're in. . .we're in the *mausoleum!*"

Rachel and Mark marched to the front of the black crypt. "After the monks kill their victims, they bring 'em—"

Stephanie kicked gravel on the floor. "Don't touch it." She was shaking. "Can we get outta here and go somewhere else? I think I'm gonna puke if I stay here a second longer!"

Larry pushed her out, and they retraced their steps.

At the bottom of the stairs, Mark said, "Where the tunnel split five ways, we'll go to our right this time." He waved them forward.

Three-quarters of the way down that fourth passageway, Rachel chuckled, "This is almost as long as the Lincoln Tunnel."

Mark examined the walls with his light. "It's also bigger than the other one. Must be ten feet all around."

Larry asked, "We're going due east, aren't we?"

Rachel rubbed the back of her neck. "Yeah, I think so. We're probably under Nicky's Field, headed toward Knights Hall."

Larry whispered to Stephanie, "You all right?" She gave him a weak smile; he hugged her.

Stephanie felt for her knife in her pocket. "No monks on patrol?"

The others grumbled.

"Up ahead." Mark extended the flashlight. "Stairs."

"I hope we don't find any more coffins!" Stephanie whispered.

At the top of the stairs, they reached a door that, when Mark turned the brass knob, opened a crack. He slid it all the way open and ran the light around the room.

Tugging on his shirt from behind, Rachel asked in a low voice, "What's there?"

"A carpenter's delight."

Once they were inside, Mark stuck his head out the door, looked both ways, and said, "Nobody followed us."

But moving down the hallway they had run through the other night, they heard a voice call out from behind them, "Hey! You four! Where do you think you're going?" The monk was holding a club.

"Shit! *Run!*" They sprinted toward another door that was

halfway open.

"In here," Mark whispered. Once inside, he slid all the latches shut, pulled a length of rope from his pocket and tied it around the doorknob, and a latch on the top, as tight as possible. Picking up his flashlight, he leaned back against the door.

Rachel asked, "Mark, what the hell are you doing? We have to hide."

"I feel like I've traveled through time to the Dark Ages. Get a load of this stuff."

As Rachel was about to say something, there came a pounding on the door. "You're mine!"

They scattered deeper into the room.

Moments later, the door flew open, and in staggered the monk. "You can't hide forever."

Kneeling behind a pot of oil, Stephanie felt something crawl over her shoes. The creature's chattering noise made her feel sick all over.

"Once I find you," the monk stood next to the stretcher, "I'm going to give you such a beating."

Stephanie started screaming when the rat touched her leg. She reached behind, grabbed the animal by its hairy tail, and flung it at the monk, who dropped his weapon.

The guys charged at him, knocking him onto the stretcher. His mask popped off and landed near the iron maiden.

Rachel turned to Mark. "It's—let's get *out* of here!" They ran through the open door and retraced their steps faster than they'd ever run in their lives.

# CHAPTER 11

WHEN PROFESSOR DRAKE SLAMMED THE DOOR, his Ancient Philosophy class quieted down. He propped a painting of men dressed in togas on the chalk rack of the old blackboard behind his desk. "Good afternoon," he announced, taking off his jacket and setting his briefcase on the floor. "Continuing our discussion of Socrates." Six feet tall, with reddish hair and thin eyebrows, he stepped off the dais, heading to Rachel near the vertical windows. "He died for what he believed in." He gestured to the 1787 *Death of Socrates* by David. The bare-chested philosopher in beard and mustache, sitting on a bed, willfully accepts the hemlock while his devastated peers surround him. "Isn't that right, Miss Yards?"

She nodded.

Scratching the pointed chin that anchored his V-shaped face, he declared, "No matter what is at stake, a leader of a cause will die for what he or she believes in." He stared at her.

"Yes." He came so close she had to swing her legs to the side.

"When opposing forces meet, there'll be a fight to the death."

He seized her desk. "Don't you agree?"

"Absolutely." She blinked at the edge of the tattoo underneath his watch.

"Good." He retreated to the dais, where he described Socrates' beliefs and those of the ones who had opposed him.

She rolled her eyes at Mark.

A few rows behind them, two girls, The Tree and Fatso, were grumbling: They knew Professor Drake liked Rachel and were disgusted by how obvious it was. Hating him and Wells for always calling on her in class, they had felt justified starting a rumor that Rachel was into witchcraft after seeing two guys in robes and masks flying out of her room.

The heavyset one with a round face, next to the cinderblock wall, leaned toward her taller friend. "She always wears a miniskirt for him."

They giggled.

The noise caught Rachel's attention, and she sneered at them.

As he was writing *Know Yourself* on the whiteboard, Drake winced. "Professor, what's wrong?" asked the guy next to Rachel. "You look like you're in pain."

Drake smiled grimly. "I, ah, tripped in the bathroom."

Mark covered his mouth: The man had been reaching for his abdomen for most of the class.

For forty minutes, Drake filled the whiteboard with notes on Socrates. When the bell rang, he said, "Tomorrow we study those influenced by him." The students piled out.

Bumping Rachel, Fatso muttered, "Witch!"

Rachel glared at her. "What is your *problem?*"

"*You* are, sweetheart." The Tree followed her friend into the hallway.

Before Rachel and Mark left the classroom, Drake cleared his throat. "Hold on, you two." He put on his jacket. "Remember! Loose lips sink ships."

Rachel smiled. "Thanks for the advice, Professor." Going down the stairs, she said under her breath, "I have an idea."

An hour after dinner, Rachel and Stephanie were in their dorm, working at their computers, when they heard a knock at the door. "Who is it?"

"It's Ralph. I'm here with Barbara and Marvin."

Rachel unlocked the door. "Come in."

Barbara came in first. Rachel extended her hand to a smiling African American freshman of medium build and her own height, wearing glasses. "Rachel Yards. Pleased to meet you."

"Marvin Koleman. Likewise."

"That's Stephanie Brooks. You can all sit on her bed."

While Barbara sat there and started chatting with Stephanie, the boys looked around the half-dark room; Nirvana was playing on the radio. The sheets on Rachel's bed had been rolled into a ball, and a bra occupied the place where the pillow should have been. On her desk, papers and books lay criss-crossed every which way. Shoes were scattered over the floor. Stephanie's desk was spotless, her bed as if it had never been slept in. Ralph chuckled. "Who are you two? A female version of the Odd Couple?"

Marvin glanced at the posters on either side of the window above Rachel's bed—an advertisement for Seaside Heights, and near the corner, a promotional poster for *The Raven*, a silent movie filmed in Fort Lee. "I take it you're from Jersey."

"Toms River."

Ralph asked, "How do you deal with toxic waste? You a Bon Jovi fan?"

Rachel grabbed his shirt. "You want to get hit?"

Stephanie waved the thought away. "Don't mind her."

Ralph sat down. "Sorry."

Stephanie nudged her mouse with her elbow. "She's grumpy because she's been through a lot lately."

"What?" Barbara crossed her legs. "Term papers? Job interviews?"

Stephanie smiled. "She was chased across campus, she was almost crushed to death, and she was the target of a violent attack."

Marvin stared at Ralph. "What the hell have you gotten me into?"

The door opened again. "Hey, Mark." Rachel kissed him. "What's up, Larry?" She closed the door.

Barbara smoothed strands of hair behind her ear. "I heard you're into witchcraft."

Rachel shook her head. "What's this *witch* business? Who started that rumor?"

Settling on Rachel's bed, Mark said, "Yeah, there's a rumor going around."

"Great." Rachel pointed at the door. "I bet those two bitches down the hall started it. Fatso and the Tree. Fatso shoved me at the end of the Philo class."

Larry chuckled, "You cast spells. Talk to ghosts."

"Ghosts?" Marvin exclaimed.

Barbara asked, "Stephanie, how did you and Rachel meet?"

Stephanie lifted her glasses to rub her eyes. "Freshmen year, in Intro to Communications, we started talking about radio in a time of downloading. Birds of a feather. We've done internships at local radio stations and in the City."

As Rachel moved across the floor, Ralph followed her, but looked away when she sat down and crossed her legs.

Marvin tapped his knee. "You guys sound great on our campus radio."

Rachel nodded. "Ralph tells me you're a trustworthy guy." She smiled at the three newcomers. "We asked you to come here tonight because we need your help. We also ask you not to discuss this with any of your friends. We...uh, we have good reason to believe there's a secret society operating here, and that they've kidnapped and murdered certain students who don't fit their mold, like Sarah and Melvin." She saw a wall of seriousness descend over their young faces. "Have any of you ever heard the Clock Tower story?"

Ralph and Marvin nodded; Barbara shook her head. Rachel took a few minutes to tell her. When she finished, Marvin asked, "What about these ghosts?"

From across the room, Mark said, "Rachel scared one in Temple Hall."

Rachel shrugged. "I'm guessing, now, that they're former members of a secret society who felt the group had gone too far, and probably got killed for it."

"...Why don't you talk to the police?" Barbara finally asked. "I mean about Mel and Sarah, anyway."

Stephanie coughed. "We have. They said the case is closed, since their bodies were found along with those of the other victims of the Woodsman Killer. And they're also stretched thin because of the emphasis on anti-terrorism prevention. My father—he's in the defense bar—was ready to sleep here if they hadn't caught that guy." Suddenly, she grew thoughtful. "Now that I think of it, he knows the chief of police in King of Prussia. Maybe he could give us some insight. I'll email him."

Ralph raised a finger. "I heard stories about ghosts roaming Temple and Davis Hall. I asked my history teacher, Marsh, about 'em, but he said it's nonsense."

Rachel crossed her legs the other way. "That's how you can help us. We need you to speak to a few people. We want you, Ralph, to talk to Dean Sands about the power of the Constitution and the beauty of Western philosophy."

The youngster sat back. "I can do that."

"Good." Rachel pointed at Barbara. "We need you to talk to Wells. He helped you with your stomach virus. Ask him how the school got its name."

"I've been curious about that myself. I have an English professor named Castle."

"Marvin—see what you can find out from that Stalin lookalike, Heglan, at the library."

Barbara was twirling a lock of her hair, sneaking looks at Mark and Larry. ". . .How did you four get involved in this?"

Rachel cleared her throat. "I was in the wrong place at the wrong time."

Ralph squeezed the mattress, forcing Stephanie to shift in her seat. "When do we get to join your wild adventures?"

Rachel smiled. "One step at a time."

Friday morning in the rain, books in one hand, an umbrella in the other, Ralph shouted over the wind and thunder, "Excuse me, Dean Sands."

"Yes, son?" The well-dressed man carrying a briefcase and umbrella smiled and paused on a stretch of black pavement that cut through grass and trees extending from Knights Hall to the other buildings and parking lots. Some of that grass had already become waterlogged. "What can I do for you?"

Ralph moved to the edge of the path. "My teachers suggested I speak—"

Sands raised his briefcase. "Let's talk in Bishop Hall, get out of the rain." He waved him to the gray gothic building. The stone entrance jutted forward, with towers on each side. Beyond that stood Jon's Hall, a dorm that rose twenty floors.

Inside the lobby, they shook hands, and Sands asked, "How can I help you?"

"I'm Ralph Ford." The youngster glanced at the raindrops on the glass doors. "Since I'm thinking about majoring in constitutional law with a minor in Western philosophy, my teachers suggested I speak to you."

"Excellent! The U.S. Constitution is the backbone of America, you know. It and the Declaration of Independence. Sacred documents. Great ideas. Defend them to the death."

Ralph stepped back involuntarily.

Sands raised a hand. "I didn't mean to scare you. But they, and the memory of men like George Washington and Alexander Hamilton, are constantly under attack from liberals, socialists, environmentalists. . . . Something must be done to rid the world of those scoundrels!" A clap of thunder stopped him. "I'll make a list of names for you." Sands bent to unsnap his briefcase and handed the boy a sheet of paper. When he opened the door, the wind made the sheets on the bulletin board dance, covering the plaque of Professor

Bishop. "Have a good day."

Ralph ran a hand through his hair. "Thanks."

On the first floor of Knights Hall, Dean Sands called out, "Rachel! Stephanie!"

They had come down a nearby stairwell.

He raised his voice. "I just had a conversation with your friend Ralph Ford. He asked me about the Constitution and Western philosophy. You put him up to talking to me for any reason?"

Rachel shrugged. "We're communications majors. If he had any questions about his courses, we would've told him to speak to the freshmen dean."

Sands covered his chin. "The boy did mention he spoke to his teachers. . . . All right, run along." He turned to the elevator.

In the noisy cafeteria, a downpour was clattering the vertical windows. Marvin spotted the librarian assistant eating with a pear-shaped woman, a co-worker. As he neared them, she picked up her tray and said goodbye. Passing each other, they smiled. "Excuse me, Mr. Heglan. I'm sorry to interrupt your meal." A steaming bowl of vegetable soup and crackers sat before the man. "But I'm looking for a book on torture. I'm curious about what drove the Woodsman Killer to kill those people the way he did."

The man wiped his mouth with a napkin. "Poor teaching at home."

Marvin leaned his umbrella on an empty chair. "I thought that kind of torture ended in the Middle Ages."

"Some things never go out of style."

The freshman sank onto a chair. There was a long pause before he asked, "How long have you been here?"

"Thirty years."

"Thirty. . . . You should be the director!"

Dipping a cracker in his soup, Heglan said, "I'm satisfied with my position."

Studying the man's hard-edged face, Marvin thought Rachel had been correct. He *did* look like Stalin. "What's changed here in all that time?"

The man rubbed his lips. "Well, every state's represented now. There's a more diverse student body. School's added more dorms and enlarged the parking lots."

Marvin nodded. "Thirty years. . . . You must've seen them film *The Omen* here."

Heglan shrugged. "I was too busy inside the library to know."

"You didn't see *anything?*"

Checking his watch, Heglan said, "I heard she was destined to die. I mean that black dog was a demon."

Marvin, noticing ink marks underneath the guy's Seiko and a rose gold Yale ring. "You think you can find books on torture by tomorrow?"

"Stop by the front desk at noon."

"Thanks." Marvin picked up his umbrella. "Enjoy your lunch."

In a drizzle by Freemun's Pond later that afternoon, Barbara stumbled against Wells. "Professor!"

The plump man grabbed her by the elbow. "I got you. Steady."

"Thanks. I'm Barbara Quorke," the redhead announced. "I'd . . .I'd like to thank you for helping me the other night. I had a stomach virus."

He nodded as they passed a bench. "Oh, yes. Glad to've been of service."

Bumping umbrellas, she said, "Oh! I'm sorry. . . . You know I'm working on an essay for English class, 'What's In a Name'? And it made me think. How did the University get its name?"

Grinning, Wells said, "The governor's nephew was a master at chess. The game takes planning, strategy, and patience. One of the pieces is a knight. And knights are powerful, brave, and committed to one cause, like academic excellence. Hence the name."

"Really."

"Who's your English teacher?"

"Castle."

He nodded. "Can I be of any further assistance?" When she shook her head, he said, "Bye, now," and turned right.

In the commuters' lounge on the second floor of the Marshall Complex, Rachel was tapping away at her laptop with Stephanie sitting next to her when Barbara dropped off a folded note an hour after she spoke to Wells. The girl continued down the walkway, past tables, chairs, and couches on both sides toward the offices. Rachel whispered, "These freshmen are good."

Flipping open the note, Stephanie said, "It worked out perfectly. Marvin and Ralph gave their info to the guys in the gym. . . ." She handed it to Rachel.

Rachel placed it next to the others. "I told you it would."

Coming from the west end of the building, the formal dining area, The Tree and Fatso asked in unison, "Whatcha doing in the commuter lounge, Rachel? Testing out another spell?"

Rachel grumbled, "Since the two of you have infected the floor of our dorm, we had to study here."

They mumbled their way to the elevator.

Rachel cracked her knuckles. "Other key words. 'Defend the

Constitution to the death. Rid the world of scoundrels.'" She glanced at the note. "'She was destined to die. Powerful, brave, committed to one cause.'"

Stephanie looked out the window. "It's stopped raining. I can see the sun peeking out between the clouds."

Rachel snapped her computer shut. "We can go now."

Back at the dorm, the girls asked, "What the hell is that?" A witch sitting on a broom, looking as if it had crashed into something, was nailed to their door. Spray-painted above it, they read *Rachel—The Witch*.

Stephanie said, "Let's burn it."

"No." Rachel crossed her arms. "We may find a use for it."

# CHAPTER 12

F LINGING HIS READING GLASSES onto a file on his desk labeled *R. Yards*, Dean Sands barked, "Nailing that devilish decoration to your door, and the spray paint, will cost you. That's school property you damaged."

Rachel sat up in the armchair across from him. "I didn't do it. It was probably Fatso and her tall friend down the hallway."

"Oh?" A smile flickered over his thick lips and erased the lines on his forehead. "That's how you refer to your classmates?" The glow returned to his brown eyes. "What do you call her friend?"

Rachel frowned. "The Tree."

The man laughed. "They must call you The Witch. That's how you see ghosts." He scribbled something on the papers in front of him. "I should be playing golf this morning. Instead I'm. . . ."

Rachel was looking past him—at the packed bookcases, the silent computer on the credenza, the certificates, plaques, framed pictures, and other documents on the walls, the long curtains, the unobstructed view of Davis Hall and the dorms. A small refrigerator sat in the near corner. The school's emblem hung on the wall in the far one, above the flagpoles. "This is a lavish office you have here, nicer than O'Connor's."

"That's *President* O'Connor to you. . . . I hear you and Mark Lexington have been bothering him about your mythical monks."

She shrugged. "I'm sure you know all about them."

He studied her with pursed lips. "You are persistent, aren't you? Well, these next three weeks—what with finals, field trips, award dinners, senior week, graduation—should keep you busy."

"And if it doesn't?" She winked.

"Then don't blame me if things go bump in the night."

She brought her chair to the edge of his desk. "How could you let such unthinkable things happen here?"

He leaned forward. "I believe in structure, Ms. Yards. Discipline. Living by a code, maintaining order, following orders, tradition."

"Even if that means. . . ." She burst into tears.

He sat back. "Stop bullshitting me, Rachel." After a few moments, he added, "Oh, calm down. Take this." He offered her a tissue. "Why are you such a maverick?"

After she blew her nose and wiped away her tears, she sighed, "When I was in high school, I dated this boy who had a troubled home life. Things got so bad, he ran away from home one day and was never heard from again. The local police told me there are too many undesirables out there who take advantage of young kids, turning them into drug addicts, or criminals—or kill 'em." She coughed. "Growing up with three older brothers, I got bounced around some. But they taught me how to change a tire, climb the docks at the bay. I knew how to drive a car at fourteen. I could handle beer a year before that." She noticed the Yale ring on his finger.

"Impressive." He slipped a breath mint into his mouth. "You might not understand this today, but years from now, when you're a deejay at a radio station and the ratings are slipping because the audience wants to hear *other* music that angers you, and your bosses change the formats, you'll understand."

She shook her head. "I'll never understand *this*, and I hope to change it."

"That's too bad for you, Rachel." He rose and slowly moved around the desk. "You're an ideal student for this university. Fabulous grades. Varsity athlete. Wonderful deejay. You'll be winning an award in two weeks." He pushed back his in-tray to sit on the corner of the desk. "And you're a beautiful young woman."

Halfway out of the chair, she grabbed his hands. "Can't you stop this?"

He shook his head. "I have no choice. I could easily disappear, just like Mark could."

She fell back.

Towering over her, he snapped, "Ah, the great Rachel Yards has a weakness—her close companions. You and Mark should get married, have kids, and play a lot of rock music."

She eased herself up. "Dean Sands, I'm going to wear an outfit specifically for you at the awards dinner that will spin your head." She looked deep into his eyes. "You're turning red."

The door opened, and in walked the dean's lively, rotund secretary. "Excuse me, John."

He eased Rachel back a step. "Ms. Yards was just on her way out."

Rachel kept smiling.

He took another breath mint. "You'll receive a bill in the mail for the damages."

She blew him a kiss.

When she closed the door, he shook his head. "Women create such a terrible distraction."

The secretary clasped her hands. "She likes you, but you're too old for her. . . . You should go back to dating, you know. It's been years since the divorce."

"Gloria," he sighed, "why'd you come in here?"

"To remind you that next Saturday night is the governor's dinner. It will include most of the administration and faculty. The governor will be here for the annual awards."

Rachel had her ear to the other side of the door. The comment about women and the dinner widened her smile.

Later that afternoon, nearing the doorway of the Marshall Complex, Barbara broke away from a group of girls to join Larry and Mark. Their shadows extended from the cement to the knight statues below the second floor windows. "Hi, guys. Where's Rachel and Steph?"

Larry shrugged. "They weren't ready for dinner yet, so they told us to go ahead."

Twisting a strand of her red hair, Barbara said, "The last time my friends and I went into Suffern to shop, Wells was talking to two men in suits, carrying briefcases. I saw them go into a Dunkin' Donuts."

"Really."

"Yep." She kicked her leg back. "I don't know what it means." Hearing her friends calling to her from inside the building, she shouted, "Be right there."

Mark asked, "Any of 'em look familiar?"

She shook her head. "I've never seen them before, but I'll keep my eyes open." She left.

"What's up, guys?" Mark and Larry turned around to see Rachel and Stephanie approach them.

"Wasn't that Barbara?" Rachel asked.

Mark put his arm around her. "She told us she saw Wells talking to some men while she was in Suffern."

Rachel's eyes widened. "That's interesting. Wells' appointment book had an entry that read 'meeting with T. A.'"

"We're going in," said Larry. "We'll find a table."

"Okay." Rachel asked, "Why was she so excited?"

"Because she's helping us."


THE NEXT DAY, Rachel was eight minutes into her afternoon radio shift from one to five. Headphones on, she flipped a switch and, speaking into the microphone below the On the Air sign, said, "What's up, Knights University? This is Rachel Yards on 101.4, WKHU, on Sunday, May 1. When I was a kid, we used to say 'April showers bring May flowers.' And the flowers are blooming on campus. I'm here again to spin another four hours of grunge rock for you. To start this set, here's 'Man In The Box,' by Alice-In-Chains." She took off the headphones to hug Stephanie, who had slipped into a chair by the control panel. "What's happening?"

"A few things." Stephanie crossed her legs. "I was studying the reports we got from Wells' office and I noticed a T. A. on them, too. It might be someone, or something, important, like the big bosses. Wouldn't be the feds, because he's one of the monks. Wells's probably been giving T. A. reports on you."

Rachel laughed. "Tomorrow, after class, we should go to the library to see whether a girl hanged herself about thirty years ago. Check out if there's anything behind the rumor about *The Omen*."

"What time tomorrow?"

"My last class is at three, so how about we meet four-thirty, in front?" Rachel snapped her fingers. "Also, this Saturday night would be perfect to go up to the clock tower. Sands and most of the admin people are going to Albany for a dinner. I forgot to tell you." She touched buttons to adjust the bass.

"What's your plan?"

Rachel shrugged. "We'll use the tunnels and take it from there."

Stephanie looked up at the off-white ceiling and the black speakers in the corner. "You really think there's documents up there?"

Headphones on again, Rachel nodded and leaned into the mike. "Before we break for station ID, it's time for the weather." She glanced at a computer. "This afternoon we'll have a mixture of sun and clouds, with gusts to ten miles an hour, a mild fifty-five degrees, and a possible thunder storm tonight, so get out your rain gear, guys." She flipped more switches on the control panel.

Stephanie said, "I got an e-mail from my dad. His friend and Lieutenant Otto are talking about Sarah and Mel. Hey, where's Mark?"

Rachel checked her watch. "He should be here soon."

"I have laundry to do anyway. Oh. This should make you happy. Fatso and the Tree went home for the weekend. Dinner at five-thirty?" After a thumbs-up from Rachel, Stephanie left.

Leaning back, Rachel thought she heard someone at the door. "Mark?"

He popped in a minute later. They embraced with kisses. "I saw Steph on the stairs."

Rachel played with his goatee. "She went to do laundry."

Mark motioned behind him. "Rachel, you should lock the door with these monks floating around—"

A knock surprised them. "Come in?"

"Hi, guys." Barbara rushed in, grabbed a chair, and crossed her legs. "I've never been in a radio station before. This is cool." Her cell rang.

Rachel spoke into the microphone. "I haven't played this in a while." Nirvana's "Smells Like Teen Spirit" filled the airwaves.

Smiling, Barbara said, "My friends want to go shopping, so maybe next time you can show me the station." She left the chair where it was. "I'll talk to you guys later." She tore out of the room.

"Rachel. Rachel?" Mark poked her in the ribs. "Hello."

"What?" She was glaring at him again.

"What are you mad about?"

Rachel grumbled, "The way she was all over you. I didn't think you liked girls with freckles and braces!"

"Rachel! I can't believe you're jealous!" He shook her. "She's a kid. You're the only woman for me." They were about to kiss when there was another knock at the door. "Yes?"

"What's up, guys?" Ralph moved the chair next to her. "This is a cool set-up." He pointed at the controls.

Rachel asked, "What can we do for you, Ralph?"

"I was wondering if—" he grabbed her elbow— "if I could help you get those documents in the clock tower. Spy on Sands for you. Review the courses given at this university."

"First off, may I have my arm back?" She smiled. "How about

you research the funding for this school?"

"Great. Anything for you, Rachel." He kissed her fingers. "Later." He left.

Rachel turned white.

Mark put his arm around her. "You have a bigger problem than the monks."

She lowered the volume. "Here's Stone Temple Pilots singing 'Plush.'"

Moments later, the doorknob began turning. . .then stopped.

A minute went by. There was another knock at the door. "Come in."

Marvin entered. "Hi! Can I join you?" He pointed to the chair. "This seat is warm."

They laughed. "What's on your mind?"

"The night you invited me and the others to your dorm got me thinking."

Rachel interrupted him to give the news and weather.

He told stories he had heard of gang torture.

Rachel broke in again to say. "Talking to friends about serious topics, this seems appropriate." She played "Black Hole Sun" by Soundgarden.

His final remark cheered them up. "You can count on me for anything to defeat this secret society. What's my next assignment?"

Rachel sat up. "Talk to Professors Drake and Castle. See if you can get any info from them."

"Will do." He shook their hands and left.

Rachel tapped Mark's knee. "He's a good kid. Speaking of professors, you and Larry should talk to your accounting professor, because it was a really tall guy who attacked me at the library. And this Saturday night we're gonna search for the—" She noticed the doorknob turning. "Marvin? Did you forget something?"

Mark jumped off the seat and flung the door open. He didn't see or hear anyone in the hallway. Marvin had already gone down the stairs. Mark marched up to a door across the hall labeled *Staff*. It was locked. He returned, taking a deep breath. The lines were disappearing from his forehead, and he was no longer snarling.

"Anything?"

He shook his head. He let her finish talking into the microphone before he tugged at her hair. "Listen, you and I are a team, okay? Ralph and Barbara will calm down sooner or later. And let's try to avoid the monks at all costs." He kissed her. "See you at dinner." He closed the door behind him.

Meanwhile, in a supply room of Knights Hall between the torture chamber and the carpenter's shop, five crows were squawking in cages, and a tall monk, whip in hand, was asking a shorter one, putting a butcher's knife on a shelf next to swords, "Well? Anything to report?"

"She had visitors her entire shift. It was like a doctor's office. I couldn't get near her. Lexington almost caught me."

The master cracked the whip on the floor. "Damn it. That girl has more lives than a cat."

# CHAPTER 13

STEPHANIE RETRIEVED A FOLDED SHEET of paper from her front pocket. "Rachel, I almost forgot. I got an e-mail from my dad this morning. There were some differences between Sarah and Mel and the other victims of the Woodsman Killer."

"Like what?"

Stephanie put sun clips on her glasses. "Let's see. . . seven out of the ten victims were in their thirties. One guy was twenty-eight. Most were good-looking, too. Sarah and Mel weren't. And the other women had been raped. She hadn't. Sarah and Mel had their wrists and ankles tied together, like the rest, and the manner of stabbing was the same, but they'd been whipped across the back, too."

Rachel kicked a rock along the asphalt path. "No one wondered about the discrepancies?"

"Rachel—" Stephanie put the sheet away— "remember how the people in Suffern and the neighboring towns were up in arms for the police to catch this guy? *Any* guy?" A squirrel ran past them. "Gus Clement was it."

Rachel sighed. "And since he's a psycho, he probably enjoyed taking credit for the other two murders. Still, I've read enough true crime to know the difference. Remember the Lindbergh kidnapping? An HBO movie showed how that German guy was framed. The carpenter got his hands on the ransom money. The Jersey State police were forced to arrest someone."

Stephanie turned to her. "Maybe he went along with it. Was paid off? My dad says that he and his friend will keep looking into it."

Rachel popped a bubble. "If we could get our hands on some of the tools our buddies used, we could prove—"

"Hey, does the name look familiar?" Stephanie whispered at the foot of the library steps.

Rachel gazed up at the gray stone building. "Schmidt Library. The professor who wrote the diary we found."

In the reference room, Rachel typed *universitytimes.com* into a computer near front windows decorated by knights. Sunlight was pouring in. Waiting for the information to come up on the screen, they glanced at the over-sized Atlas books on shelves near the wall. "The football stadium looks small from here, but I can see the guys' dorm window."

"Scary, isn't it?" The site came on. Rachel clicked on back issues for the year 1975. She came across the headline *Knights University Opens Door to Female Students*. "We'll start from here." After scrolling down a while, the article "Women Protest Inequality on Campus," from October 1976, caught her attention. "I think we've found what we're looking for." She read: "'The protest dealt with paucity of courses aimed at women. The newspaper is written from a male point of view. Women are treated as second-class citizens and are housed in the oldest dorms!'" She skimmed past the next few lines. "'Valerie Perry, founder of Order of Women, led the protest. Weeks before the march on campus, she had written letters to the editor on the subject.'"

Stephanie pointed to the screen. "'Two nights later, Valerie Perry hanged herself outside her window at Welch Hall. Doctors found drugs and alcohol in her system. A spokesman for the administration said, "Valerie's group, and the protest, put Ms. Perry under tremendous pressure. Her suicide reminded me of *The Omen* when the nanny hanged herself."'" Three lines down, she continued. "'Police ruled the incident a suicide because of a note and drugs in her room. The girl had a prescription for amphetamines.'"

Rachel turned to her. "That's probably how the rumor started."

Stephanie whispered, "Sarah Appleton was a member of Order of Women."

From behind them, Wells asked, "Is what you girls are doing related to your classwork?" The girls jumped. "Sorry. I was checking to make sure you weren't using the Internet for nonsense. That costs the university money."

Rachel sighed. "I'm researching secret societies for my final paper."

"I'm helping her."

"Very well, then." He huffed off.

Stephanie waved her hand in the air. "Talk about bad breath."

Rachel typed in *T. A.* "One of the monks who attacked me had bad breath. . . . Tony Awards. Trent Affair. Triple Alliance. We still don't know what T. A. is." She typed in *clock tower.* "Where do you think the papers are hidden? In the clock? The weathervane?"

Stephanie had been playing with her bracelet. "What makes you think they're still up there?"

Rachel grumbled, "I'm counting on it. Otherwise, we don't have a prayer."

"Rachel!" Ralph put his hand on her shoulder. "I got news for ya!"

At the end of the row, an older woman yelled, "Young man, this is a library. We'll have no more outbursts like that!"

"Sorry." He sat down. "Besides alumni donations," he whispered, "the school gets money from J. P. Morgan Chase, Citigroup, Goldman Sachs, American Express, and a bunch of other big companies."

"Really!" She tapped his hand. "Why don't you research what was here before they built this university."

"Okay. See ya around."

Stephanie leaned back. "He's got a crush on you."

Rachel whispered, "It's worse than that." She sat up. "And Barbara has the hots for Mark."

"Speaking of Mark—" Stephanie pushed in the chair— "we're supposed to meet the guys soon."

Rachel logged off.

When the girls left the room, Wells put a disk into the hard drive of the computer they had been using.

In the Marshall Complex, sunlight was ending shy of their cafeteria table. Mark asked Rachel, "Ralph still hovering around you?"

"Yes." Rachel stabbed at her meatloaf. "We were in the library." She took a bite, immediately began to cough, and spit the food out of her mouth.

"Rachel!" The three jumped out of their seats.

She waved them off. "This is horrible. It tastes like it's three days old." She drank her Coke. "Blah. Sludge." Wiping her mouth with a napkin, she put her arm around Mark. "Sweetie, can you get me. . . ."

"Anything for you, beautiful." He took her tray and motioned for Larry to join him.

At that moment, someone covered Rachel's eyes from behind.

"Ralph!" Stephanie exclaimed. "What are you doing?"

"Hi, girls." He turned to the center of the room. "I got something for you." He unfolded a sheet of paper.

"Wait!" Stephanie stood up, pointing. "Check out the garbage can where Mark threw your food." A noxious smelling vapor had begun to rise from it, and a roach had climbed up and was sitting at the edge, antennas jerking. Moments later, it fell dead on its back.

Fatso, who had been eating near the garbage can, ran toward the entrance. A chorus of laughter arose. A janitor with a ring of keys at his hip started cleaning up the mess.

Returning to the table, Rachel said, "I think someone just tried to *kill* me!" Sinking onto her chair, she looked at Ralph. "What did you want to show me?"

"Here." He handed her a drawing.

Her mouth fell open. "*Thank* you!"

Mark slid a tray of food across to her.

"Whatta ya think?" Ralph was swaying side to side. "That oval face, the brown eyes and black hair, puffy cheeks, angled eyebrows, pointy nose—all characteristic of a witch. What saves you is that flat chin. Most witches have pointy ones."

"Pointy nose?" She touched it. "Mine is round."

He waved his arm. "I haven't figured out what was here before they built this university, but Rachel," he whispered, and leaned over her, "when are we going to search for ghosts?"

"Tomorrow night. After dark, we'll hunt for them in Davis Hall."

Ralph smiled. "Just the two of us?"

"No. I don't go anywhere without these three."

"Call me." Ralph left.

Mark put his arm around her. "What'd he give you?"

She handed him the drawing.

Larry asked, "What was all the screaming about?"

Stephanie swallowed a piece of meatloaf and told him. Looking at Rachel, she said, "You're brave!"

"I'm hungry." Rachel inspected the roast beef.

"Hi, guys." Barbara had come over and leaned on Mark's shoulders.

Shifting in her seat, Rachel rested her ear on her fist. "What's up, Barbara?"

The other girl did not move. "I've been thinking about what Wells told me by the pond. The names of the buildings sound like *people*, not chess pieces. If the governor's nephew liked the game so much, why are the school's colors gray and not black or red? There are no pictures of this guy anywhere, just framed photos of knights here in the café, upstairs in the commuter lounge, in the library, in the gym. Who's Nicky's Field named after? And the radio station's call letters are WKHU. What does HU stand for? Shouldn't it be WKUH?"

Taking a deep breath, Rachel said, "That's wonderful thinking! Keep it up. Aren't you hungry?" She kicked Mark's leg.

"Not really."

Stephanie asked, "Barbara, where'd ya get those bracelets?"

"Suffern. . .I better go. See ya tomorrow."

When she left, Mark kissed Rachel. "Hey, it's nothing."

Stephanie was polishing her glasses with a napkin. "Anyway, she did have some valid points. The names of the buildings. . .except for Freemun's Hall, there are no photos of the governor's nephew. And what *does* the 'HU' stand for?"

Chewing, Rachel mumbled, "I've been thinking about that. Harvard U?"

Larry and Stephanie both smiled when they saw Marvin approach. "Here's our other recruit," she said.

He marched by without saying a word but dropped a note on the table.

Rachel picked it up. "Why didn't he stop to say hello?" The four lost sight of him when he entered the kitchen. She opened it up to read, at just above a whisper, "'Professor Drake, a very distant relative of Sir Francis Drake, the British explorer, claims that England is the most civilized country in the world. Wherever they went, the British brought a notion of civilization to the inhabitants. People who resisted their customs and philosophy were stupid. America was lucky to have had men like Washington and John Adams to lead the young nation. Liberals, socialists, the ACLU, and others have become the 21st-century adversaries of freedom, democracy, and the Constitution. Such troublemakers should watch their step. Professor Castle was tight-lipped, but he did have copies of the *National Review* and *American Heritage* on his desk." She slipped the paper into her pocketbook. "Marvin should join the FBI."

"Speaking of Drake—" Mark pointed to the kitchen— "we saw him, smoking a cigarette behind the dessert counter."

Rachel chopped her food. "Then *he* tried to poison me."

"Poison? What nonsense are you talking about now?" Dean Sands had stopped at their table, his back to the vertical windows. "I was informed of a commotion in the cafeteria. I figured I'd find you four here."

After a sip of Coke, Rachel grumbled, "Drake put some sort of poison in my food. It killed a roach."

The man in the dark suit smiled. "Rachel, you have *such* an imagination."

". . .Dean Sands," she asked, "who is Nicky's Field named after?"

"Professor Nicholas Reddington. He was an engineer who later worked on the construction of the Holland Tunnel. Brilliant man. Helped design some of the buildings here. He laid down the foundation for the university's math and engineering departments. Why the sudden interest?"

Rachel shrugged. "A friend of ours thought he was probably related to Jon Freemun, who founded the school."

Sands laughed.

Mark asked, "What's so funny?"

"Nothing." The man squared his shoulders. "Do yourself a favor and stay out of trouble. And the next time you accuse a professor of attempted murder, try to provide some solid evidence." He hurried off.

"Thanks," Rachel whispered. "Tomorrow after classes, we'll research the names of the buildings. We have exams in the morning."

Stephanie asked, "Are we really going to hunt for ghosts in Davis Hall?"

"Why not?"

# CHAPTER 14

HE CIRCULAR CLOCK ABOVE A CLASSROOM DOOR on the first floor of Davis Hall read eight P.M. The president of the club, a senior, rose, marched to the front of the room, and faced his audience. The other nineteen students and four guests quieted down. Behind him, an analysis of Dante's *Inferno*, left over from a previous class, covered the whiteboard. Above it hung a gray banner: *The Marketing Society of K. U.* "Good evening, ladies and gentlemen," he said. "Welcome to another meeting of the Society." The others clapped. The membership was evenly split between ten men and ten women, the latter including two Hispanics and one Asian. Marvin and another African American guy were there, along with Ralph and others with an interest in marketing as a career.

"For tonight's meeting," the moderator went on, brown eyes lively with excitement, "we have four deejays from WKHU who will talk about marketing on the radio." Rachel, Mark, Stephanie, and Larry were sitting by the shaded windows. Everyone clapped. "Our own Ralph Ford arranged for them to speak to us." More applause followed. "Without further ado, here is our first speaker,

Rachel Yards." The members cheered.

Rachel and Stephanie were wearing heels and knee-length skirts. The guys were in sport coats and slacks. Arms behind her back, one leg in front of the other, Rachel began. "Hello, everyone. I'm sure you know who I am, but for those of you who don't, I'm your Sunday afternoon deejay. We're here tonight to talk about marketing in radio. Despite the Internet, radio is still a huge medium for advertising. Each station, whether it's college, rock, pop, hip-hop, or dance, reaches hundreds of thousands of people every day. Remember, radio was advertising products long before television was invented."

Ten minutes later, Stephanie spoke, followed by the guys. When Larry finished, he asked, "Any questions?"

When it was over, Ralph asked, "*Now* can we hunt for ghosts?" He tossed his knapsack onto his back.

"Yes." Rachel was leaning on Mark's shoulder. "We'll start with the top floor and work our way down."

They shone their flashlights through the glass panels inset in the locked doors of the English and Communications classes. Nothing stirred. Political Science classrooms contained no ghosts or goblins either. The stairways were deserted. They avoided administrative offices. Below a window, Stephanie found an earring she'd lost the year before. Marvin found a quarter near a garbage can. A reflection along the brick wall made Larry bend down. "Huh. A ring."

Later, on the first floor, under a reproduction of Raphael's *School of Athens*, Rachel stopped to adjust her heels.

Mark asked, "You all right?"

"I'm fine. Ever since I hurt my ankle playing softball last year, these are murder on my feet."

The others gathered around her.

"Okay." Rachel looked up at *Washington Crossing the Delaware* and yelled, "Holy shit!"

Marvin covered his mouth. "Wow! A real. . .ghost."

The image of a man, missing one arm, hovered six feet off the floor with his back to them.

Mark whispered, "He's got something in his hand."

Stephanie mumbled, "The other ghost had no legs."

"They were probably tortured," Larry murmured.

"Now what?" Ralph moved toward it.

The others pulled him back.

Stephanie looked at Rachel. "You're the expert."

Marvin rubbed his arms. "Is it me, or has it gotten colder in here?"

"It's because of *him*." Rachel eased away from Mark, tapped the wall, and called out, "Is there something we can do for you?"

The ghost remained in place.

Rachel turned her head. "He's not listening to us. Mark, you're right. One shouldn't disturb—"

"*Rachel!*" Mark pointed.

The ghost had descended two feet, shifted, and was extending the document toward her. Rachel was shaking and had gone white. The creature's round, pleasant face began to turn ugly. It rose higher than the painting. Fangs emerged form its mouth. Claws formed on its hand. It growled, breaking the glass of a nearby door, and flew down the hall out the rear wall.

Screaming, Rachel dropped to the floor.

Mark carried her to a couch. After he laid her down, he

checked for a pulse. "Rachel. Speak to me." He began tapping her cheek.

On her knees, Stephanie was squeezing Rachel's hand. "Wake up!"

Larry yelled, "Ralph. Marvin. Quick! Find some water."

Ralph took off his knapsack. Removing an empty water bottle, he ran around the corner and shrieked, "Here's some!"

Mark snatched it out of the boy's hand as soon as he came back and forced Rachel to drink.

She did, greedily. ". . .Thanks."

Appearing in the hallway, President O'Connor shouted, "What the hell is going *on* here? I saw the light on—what *happened* to her?"

Rising, Stephanie gulped, "She saw a mouse."

The man stared back. "It would take a poisonous snake to scare her!" He looked around. "Someone had better tell me what *happened*." He motioned to the shattered glass. "Who damaged that door?"

Ralph stepped forward. "I. . .I did, President O'Connor. We were fooling around. I scared the hell out of them."

He nodded. "It's a pleasure to hear some honesty these days." He looked at Rachel. "Should we call the campus EMS for you?"

Tears on her face, clutching Mark, she said, "That won't be necessary. I'll be fine in my dorm."

"Okay. Help her up." Everyone but Ralph assisted her to her feet. During the exchange, Marvin slipped Larry the sheet of paper the ghost had left.

Larry said, "I'll get the door."

"You, young man." O'Connor pointed at a sniffling Ralph.

"My office. Nine A.M. sharp. Temple Hall. First floor." He stared at the two freshmen. "Both of you return to your dorms."

Outside, gazing at her shoes, arms around Mark and Stephanie, Rachel asked, ". . .Why did it *attack* me?"

Mark squeezed her waist. "Although you were helping it, I think that's what happens when a living person interacts with an angry spirit stuck in this dimension."

Rachel coughed. "Larry. What's on that sheet of paper?"

Stephanie chuckled, "She's feeling better."

Larry shone his flashlight on the documents. "It says, *NW Iron railing. Winding mechanism. North. GIC.*"

Rachel shivered. "It's the route to the papers!"

Back in Davis Hall, O'Connor called Maintenance. After a sigh, he rubbed his wrinkled face. He stared at his cell for a long time before he hit a pre-recorded button. He heard a computer voice, then a human one. "Get me Gasso."

"Yeah?"

"It's O'Connor. Things have spun out of control. The girl is getting help and still proceeding."

"*Goddamit!*" The line went dead.


THE NEXT MORNING, RACHEL SAW a depressed-looking Ralph leaving Temple Hall. "Ralph. *Ralph!*" she called out.

He lifted his head. "Rachel! Didn't recognize you with those sunglasses on. You're all smiles. I guess you've recovered from last night."

She chuckled. "I fell asleep immediately, but I dreamed that a ghost with four arms was chasing me to Freemun's Pond. When I hit the water, I woke up. Scared the shit out of Stephanie." Motioning to a bench near Loyal Hall, where the three were waiting, she added, "We'd like to thank you for sticking up for us. We owe ya." She kissed him on the cheek.

"Wow. Does this mean I can take you to the movies? I'll pay. But you have to drive."

Laughing, she said, "You'll have to talk to Mark about that. . . . What did O'Connor ask you?"

The redness on his face disappeared. "He asked me what we were doing there. I told him about the marketing club, and that we got into a conversation about philosophy. I said I was pretending I was a hockey player, checking an opponent into the boards. He said I'd have to pay for the damages. Before I left, he asked me if we saw anything strange. My answer was no, but that we heard some bizarre noises that were not human." Laughing, he continued, "You should have seen the fright and desperation on his face." He snapped his fingers. "Oh, I almost forgot." He pointed at the building with the lions and gargoyle in front. "In O'Connor's office, I saw a gap in the bookcase that looked like a secret entrance." He saw her eyebrows rise. ". . .What did the ghost give you?"

She crossed her arms. "The less you and the others know, the safer you'll be."

After classes, passing the gothic church under blue skies, Stephanie grumbled, "Rachel, stop staring at the tower. If anyone's watching us. . .we'll take the tunnels!"

"You *want* to take the tunnels?"

"You have a better idea? Anyway—" Stephanie shrugged— "I got another e-mail from my dad. Lieutenant Otto said it's strange how Mel's body was found outside the barn the Woodsman Killer used to hide the other bodies. Kids came across it when their horse got loose. They told their parents about it. Between a rash of robberies and prom season, he hasn't had time to follow up on the differences."

"You're incredible, Steph. I'm sorry."

"Forget it. When we get inside, I'll call Larry, and we'll eat."

After dinner in Shields Bar across from the cafeteria, while Stephanie and Larry were buying drinks, Mark put his arm around Rachel as they sat at a wooden table for four in the rear. The stage was bare of any instruments in the opposite corner. In the middle, a few tables were occupied. He shouted over a Hall and Oates tune, "I saw you give Ralph a kiss on the cheek this morning."

She smiled. "He wanted to take me to the movies."

"What did you say?"

"That he'd have to talk to you about that." She wiggled her fingers under his chin.

He kissed her.

"Here we go." Stephanie and Larry returned with four bottles of Budweiser. Before they sat down, Stephanie said, "We're right under the speaker. Let's move over."

Rachel and Mark sat down at the next table, with their backs to a wall decorated by school team photos. Small knight figures hung in the center of the wall.

They clicked bottles. "To ghosts and spirits!"

After a sip, Rachel lowered her head. "We on for Saturday night at the tower?"

Larry nodded. "Should we involve the freshmen?"

"No. Not for this." Rachel shook her head. "Depending on what we find, we may need them to make copies. And I've been thinking about this. If there are documents, we should send Ralph and the others to the *New York Times*."

Mark took a sip of beer. "When do we expose this discovery, assuming there's something there?"

"Night of the awards dinner."

Stephanie raised her eyebrows. "That's more than a week away. It'll be dangerous to hold onto that kind of material for so long."

Rachel nodded. "I know, but most of the admin will be away this Saturday night for a dinner in Albany. We won't get a better chance. We'll need to study the paperwork, too. We can't find any info on the Knights, Loyal, or Davis. It's like they've been erased from the database. And best of all, the governor will be here for awards night."

The others grew silent. A Madonna song had encouraged some other girls to dance.

After a long sip, Rachel said, "To avoid another diary situation, we should hold onto the material all day long, hide it in our books."

Stephanie leaned diagonally. "Have it right under their noses! I don't know if you're crazy or a genius."

Mark laughed. "A little of both."

"I'll send copies of the stuff to my dad," said Stephanie.

"I phoned my brothers to mail me the rope we used to wander through the rides at Seaside Park during the winter after we climbed over the locked fences. It should be good enough for this."

Mark shrugged. "I could call my Uncle Joe to send us some of his tools, because we'll probably need 'em up there, too."

Rachel elbowed him. "Do it."

Larry asked, "How about when we're asleep? The monks'll probably search our rooms if they know the documents have been taken."

Mark snapped his fingers. "I'll ask my uncle to throw in a couple of door chains."

Stephanie asked, "What about patrols in the tunnels?"

Rachel shrugged. "We'll work around 'em."

"What if it rains?"

Pointing to a TV screen above the bar near the ceiling, Mark cheered. "Hey, they switched to the Yankee game!"

That instant, a lamp came crashing down onto the table they had vacated. For a few moments, the light fixture dangled on the edge, then fell to the floor. Everyone stopped talking and looked in their direction. The music went off.

A bartender called out, "Are you four okay?"

"We're fine." Mark waved him over. "We could use some towels, though." Fragments of glass had flown in their direction, knocking over his bottle.

Rachel raised her bottle to Stephanie. "Good thinking before."

# CHAPTER 15

THE CROWD WENT WILD when the Princeton batter popped up the ball near second, ending the top of the first inning of the varsity softball game. "I cannot *believe* the Tree missed that tag before," Rachel exclaimed. In right field, the electronic scoreboard read *Knights 0, Visitors 2.*

Stephanie elbowed her shoulder. "You would've gotten her out."

"Thanks." Rachel glanced at Mark's diagram of the church tower. "Very good." In sunglasses and Knights' gray hats, they were sitting in the last row of the aluminum stands, with the east face of the gray gothic church ahead of them.

"Speaking of the Tree." Mark turned to the others. "Larry and I had a conversation with Professor Loom before lunch today, since we're going to the stock exchange tomorrow."

Larry said, "I asked him about security, and he said not to worry."

On the field, the Princeton players had taken their positions and were throwing softballs to one another.

Mark folded up the diagram. "Loom said the exchange is the, uh, 'last pure feature of capitalism. People complain about big business,' he said, 'but if you own stocks, you own these companies. Enroll in mutual funds or a company's 401K. Government should let the invisible hand of the market run the economy.'" A Knights batter hit a foul ball down the third-base line. "I asked him how President O'Connor was at running the university. He said, and I quote, 'He gets plenty of help.'" Pointing at Larry, Mark added, "I asked, 'Aides?' To which he answered, 'More like "advisors."'"

A diving stop of a ground ball by the Tigers shortstop, and a strong throw to first, had the visiting team cheering.

Mark smiled. "I asked him whether we get to sound the opening bell at the stock exchange. He said we probably wouldn't, but we'd get to see more movement of money than we'd ever have in our lives."

Tapping Rachel's knee, Mark added, "This is where I really got him going. I was thinking of Mel when I said I knew someone who thought the stock market was the core of sin."

The others laughed.

Mark adjusted his hat. "You should've heard him! 'Money is not evil. Greed is. That's what leads to all the scandals. Excessive demand is evil. Since there's such a demand for automobiles, houses, clothes, computers, college education, all of it, prices have naturally risen. And those who can't afford those assets probably don't deserve them. Those fortunate to have wealth and connections deserve a quality education, leading to six-figure salaries, which benefits America. Keeps the nation strong and keeps this dumbing-down of. . .anyhow,' and when he saw students showing up for his next class, he looked at his watch and said he'd see us tomorrow."

Rachel turned to Mark. "That sounds like someone willing to hold a knife to my face."

"Rachel—" Larry leaned over to her— "we noticed a tattoo under Loom's watch, too."

Rachel asked, "What's the color of his eyes?"

"Hazel." Mark snapped his fingers. "When we were talking to him, I noticed a tennis racket. I think he saw us the day we met Barbara."

Reaching for Mark, Rachel said, "I remember smelling body odor on him. . . ."

Gazing at shadow-covered left field, Rachel asked, "When was the last time we were in the church?"

"Easter."

She smiled. "Father Murray's a tough old bird."

"Hi, guys." Ralph spoke for the three freshmen who had appeared in the row below them at the bottom of the inning.

"What's up?" Rachel asked. "Anything new?"

Ralph pointed at Marvin. "He and I walked through the school cemetery last night."

Stephanie gasped. "Rachel! How on Earth did you corrupt these young men?"

"Practice." Rachel smiled. "When I was a teenager, friends of mine and I would stroll through this cemetery on Hooper Boulevard, in Silverton, north of Toms River, at night. Some of those headstones went back to the Civil War."

"Speaking of headstones," Marvin said, "we saw Knights, Temples, and Loyals, but no Freemuns or Schmidts."

A left-handed batter for Princeton drove the ball into deep right field. It made everyone stand up. She slid safely into third.

Sitting down again, Barbara asked, "What's so exciting about a cemetery? I never did that."

Rachel crossed her legs. "It's daring, and it's scary."

"It makes sense," said a guy sitting next to Larry. "Not only is that Rachel Yards the deejay, it's Rachel the Witch."

"Dave!" Rachel smiled. "Listening to my conversation?"

"Of course." The guy, who needed a shave, tipped his hat. "You still owe me a beer from last month's party." He laughed. "Mark. Larry. You might remember when my roommate and a few others carried this drunken freshman to the school cemetery last year. The kid woke up staring at a tombstone name of York. He freaked out because his last name was Tork."

They laughed.

Mark said, "Now that you mention it, I remember that story. Kid transferred to Syracuse."

"That's horrible." Barbara turned to watch Princeton score again on a short single to right.

Frowning, Dave said, "We were just joking with the kid. We got suspended for a week. My uncle tells me two guys died that way. A guy he called 'a bleeding-heart-liberal,' and a Black kid. This was the early Seventies. They got drunk at a party. Some seniors carried them to the cemetery, where they died. When we left Tork, we had him on his stomach. Those other two were found on their backs. Choked on their own vomit."

"Ugh." Stephanie shivered.

Another Princeton batter hit a pitch that almost decapitated the pitcher. A poor throw by the center fielder allowed the runners to advance to second and third.

Dave continued, "My uncle was so blasted, he thought he saw seniors, in black or brown robes, carrying those freshmen."

Marvin's eyebrows rose. "What'd the police have to say?"

"Ruled it an accidental death," Dave told him. "Campus security and school officials were involved. One guy fell out the first floor window and slept on the grass. When there was talk about people wearing robes, the admin asked if anyone had drugs. Two juniors admitted to having pot."

Barbara asked, "Did they ever find out who did it?"

Dave shook his head.

After a pop-up, a single scored one runner. Since the left fielder bobbled the ball, the other also broke for home, but the outfielder fired the ball to the plate in time to catch the runner. That ended the inning.

"Where did your uncle end up?" Rachel asked.

Dave smiled. "He fell asleep on this long Zenith TV they had back then."

"Dave?" Rachel asked, motioning. "Who put that witch decoration on our door?"

He lowered his hat. "The Tree and Fatso. I've heard them admit they miss not having you on the softball team."

"Thanks, man."

He gave her a thumbs-up.

Stephanie whispered in Rachel's ear, "Who was that?"

Rachel lowered her voice. "He's in Drake's philosophy class with me and Mark. The night I bumped into the monks, he and his friend opened the door for me."

After a Knights' batter ground out to first, Barbara asked, "Rachel, why aren't you playing softball?"

"Last year I injured my ankle sliding into home plate when this fat catcher from Saint John's fell on it. I re-injured it playing basketball this year."

A crack of the bat sending the ball to deep right field brought everyone to their feet.

After the softball game, Dean Sands saw Ralph and a friend dragging their feet on the sidewalk to Washington Hall, the dorm north of Knights Hall, their heads hung low.

"Gentlemen." Sands put his briefcase onto the sidewalk. "What's with the long faces on a beautiful day?" He shook the hand of the guy with the long neck. "Ralph Ford, correct?" He got a nod. "And you are. . . ?" He pointed to the African American with the white spot on his chin.

"Marvin Koleman."

Ralph looked at him. "Again the softball team got murdered. . . eleven to one."

Marvin agreed. "They sure could've used Rachel Yards. I bet she's the first woman astronaut to go to Mars." He glanced up at the trees and darkening sky.

Sands snickered. "She's already been there. If I were you two, I would keep my distance from Ms. Yards, because she's a troublemaker. You might consider people like her fun, but they can get you into serious trouble."

The freshman eyed each other. "Dean Sands," said Marvin, "I was reading the science section of the *Times* the other day and came across an article that quoted a Knights graduate."

The man in the dark suit smiled. "Yes. About a dozen university graduates work for NASA at either the Kennedy or Johnson Space centers. Are you thinking of a career in the space program?"

"No." Marvin gestured to Ralph. "I want to major in constitutional law, like my friend."

"That's excellent." The man's smile grew. "The weakness of the Articles of Confederation proved how important the Constitution is, and the men who created it."

Ralph asked, "Dean Sands? How come most of the teams at this school stink? No championship banners. And couldn't the admin think of a more original sports name than Swordsmen?"

The man twisted his aging lips. "Athletics are important, but here at Knights, we're more concerned with the mind. We want to prepare you for the corporate world and related fields."

Marvin shook his head. "Swordsmen is so sexist."

Sands knocked his briefcase onto its side. Not picking it up, he said, "The founding fathers of this incredible university settled on the name Swordsman for our fine male athletes long before females began coming here. And I see no reason to change it."

His cell rang. "Hello, Sands. . . . I'll be right there." He shut it off. "Sorry, guys, but I have to go. I'm late for a meeting. Been good talking to you." He grabbed his briefcase and hurried off.

Marvin smiled like it was his birthday. "Boy, will Rachel love to hear this."

Later that night, asleep in their rooms, the girls moaned when the telephone rang. Rachel jumped out of bed, slipped on a blouse, and fell back onto the mattress.

Groping to find her glasses, Stephanie mumbled, "Rachel, what are you doing?"

"Trying to answer the phone."

It rang again.

Rachel glanced at her clock next to her bed: 11:58. "The

monks are torturing us." On her knees, she picked up the receiver. "It's midnight. . . ."

"Two minutes to midnight."

"Mark?"

Looking out the window, he spoke into the receiver. "Don't you hear the clock tower bells chiming? You were right about the story. It's May, and the bells are ringing."

Rubbing her face, Rachel asked, "How come we never heard it before?"

"We weren't aware of it before. Sorry if I woke you."

On her feet, she said, "Not a problem. See ya tomorrow morning." She hung up.

Still in bed, glasses on, Stephanie said, "At least it wasn't the monks."

Rachel strolled to the window to pull back the shade. It was a star-filled sky. Under her breath, she muttered, "In forty-eight hours, we'll be in the clock tower."

"What?"

"Nothing. Good night." Rachel crawled into bed.

Still working in his office in Temple Hall, President O'Connor stopped to listen to the bells. ". . .Gordon. . . . This time your cries will be answered."

# CHAPTER 16

TIE UNDONE, WELLS APPEARED in the noisy classroom after lunch. "Sorry I'm late." He closed the door. "Lost track of time." The class quieted down. He said, "Once we complete our discussion on T. A. Eliot, we're going to move on to Auden." He started writing on the whiteboard.

"Professor Wells?" Rachel raised her hand. "Don't you mean T. S. Eliot?"

He stiffened. "You're right, Rachel. You're right." He made the correction. "Thank God it's Friday."

The students laughed.

Rachel whispered in Stephanie's ear, "T. A. again."

"And again he's late."

Later on, Rachel typed *clock tower* into a computer in the reference room, and clicked *search*. They were sitting with their backs to the windows. The sunlight threw shadows on the screens. With finals starting Monday, the room was packed. Texts and pictures of clock towers appeared.

In a low voice, Rachel read, "'Clock tower: a tower built with one or more, normally four, easily seen clock faces, usually part of a church or municipal building. Some clocks are free-standing. Yadda yadda...marks the hour by sounding bells or chimes or musical tunes. . .served an important purpose, since most people did not have watches before late in the nineteenth century. Sometimes a clock tower is the tallest edifice in a town. The best-known tower in the Western world is Big Ben, at the Palace of Westminster.'"

"Cool." Stretching strands of her hair under her nose, Stephanie suggested, "Why don't you try 'Knights University Clock Tower' in quotes?"

"Good idea." Rachel typed in the words and clicked search.

A picture of the university's clock tower and the church, along with block text, filled the screen. "'The church tower was built in 1905,'" she whispered. "'In 1964, it was outfitted with an electric motor, though it still operates mechanically. Yadda yadda. . . . Stainless steel pinion—in parentheses, toothed gear engaging with rod. Four-faced time piece. Loft hands. Cast iron carriage and supported by iron and steel platform. Glass on each dial. Blah, blah, blah. . . . Crown wheel with triangular teeth. Hour wheel. Mainspring.'" She sat back.

Stephanie read on. "Since 1965, the clock on the north side has been off two minutes. Rumors persist of cheap labor used to construct the clock tower. Most insist that isn't the case, since the workmanship is similar to that of masons. Every individual who worked on the church or on any other building at this university received fair compensation."

"In Alpine, New Jersey—" Rachel sat up— "there's a huge stone tower known as Devil's Tower, which was built by slave labor in the eighteen nineties. A wealthy South American land owner somehow smuggled slaves up north."

Stephanie said, "Cheap labor may very well have carried the tools and stones during construction."

Rachel scrolled down. "This says the clocks are fifteen feet in diameter." She clicked the back arrow.

Stephanie leaned toward Rachel. "You have any idea why this history professor would've hidden the stuff up there?"

Rachel shook her head. "Maybe he thought that was the safest place. . .or was chased in that direction. Who knows?"

When a larger shadow blocked the sunlight, Stephanie looked up. "Hi, Professor."

Rachel turned her head. "Professor Wells, we always meet in the library."

"I'm working on a research paper on the history of the indefinite third person. How's your final paper coming?"

Rachel lifted a stack of notes. "This is the last bit of research. I'll type it this weekend."

Stephanie looked up at him. "You seemed confused in class earlier, Professor."

He scratched his bald head. "This time of year is always crazy." He coughed. "Please excuse me, I must get back to my work." He walked up the aisle.

Stephanie looked down. "Rachel? What are you doing?"

"Nothing." She had pressed the power button on the hard drive twice. "I wouldn't put it past him, or the others, to track what we were searching." She waited for the screen to go from black to gray, with the rectangular sign-in box in the center. "Let's go." They pushed in their chairs to leave.

Passing the bookshelves, the two heard someone clear his

throat. Marvin led them down a path of textbooks. He indicated a stack of art volumes and disappeared around the corner.

"What is it?" Stephanie leaned on Rachel's back.

Rachel unfolded a sheet of notepaper stuck between two volumes. "More info." She slipped the note into her purse. "Ready?"

Stephanie held up a paperback. "I have to check this out."

At the circulation desk, Heglan was clearing books for a tall sophomore. The guy stared at the girls in miniskirts, making them turn to the portrait of the knights on horseback. Moments later, he left.

The Stalin look-alike snapped, "What can I do for you two?"

Stephanie put the book on the counter. "I'd like to check this out."

"Yoga? Is this supposed to make studying easier?"

Rachel crossed her arms. "Can't you do your job without the attitude?"

He titled his head at her. "You two should talk, wearing those outfits. You're dressed more for a bar than to study at a library."

Stephanie demanded, "Finished with that yet?"

"Here." He shoved it at her. "Women are such distractions."

They marched to the front door.

Stephanie grumbled, "Rude bastard."

Rachel looked at her. "Where have I heard that comment before?"

Stephanie slipped the book into her bag. "It was in Schmidt's diary."

"Ladies." The African-American security guard tipped his hat. "Is everything okay?"

They said it was. After the door closed behind them, they

paused at the top of the outer stairs, under cloudy skies and a wind that messed up their hair. "Wait." Rachel stared. "Someone else said women are distractions. But I can't remember who."

"You'll think of it." Stephanie scratched her knee. "What did Marvin say?" Stephanie asked as two crows settled on a stone railing below them.

Rachel removed the note. *In Castle's English class, a Spanish girl asked, "Are we going to read other authors besides Milton, Pope, and Ayn Rand?" His answer was, "Not within these four walls."*

"Excuse me?"

Rachel said, "Come to think of it, we read the same ones."

Another crow landed opposite the first two.

"Hello!" Ralph came running up the stone steps.

Rachel exclaimed, "What's up, Ralph?"

"Did you know Dean Sands is a huge stockholder in General Electric?"

"No."

He explained. "My father owns some, too. He saw Sands at an investors fair. . .that's not how I got accepted here. My grades, SAT scores, student council. . . ."

"Ralph! Enough!" said Rachel.

Another crow landed on the bottom part of the railing.

He smiled. "It turns out, Sands' father was the CFO of Paine Webber a long time ago. Sands did an internship there while he was at Yale. It's rumored he's a Skull and Bones guy. Later, he got a Ed. D. from Harvard. Once he earned his degree, he worked at Paine Webber too for a couple of years before coming here."

Rachel snapped her fingers. "The ring!"

"What ring?"

Rachel leaned back on the railing. "The ring I saw him wearing when I was in his office Saturday to discuss the witch on our door. It was from Yale. He strikes me as someone who *would* be a Skull and Bonesman."

Stephanie leaned closer to Ralph. "How'd you get this info on Sands?"

He said, "When my father called me last night to figure out when he and my mom were going to pick me up, I told him about Sands."

Rachel chuckled, "Maybe next week, I'll take you up on that offer for a movie."

"Great." He ran into the library.

Rachel raised a finger. "It was *Sands* who said 'women are distractions.'"

Stephanie's face grew pale. "Rachel. What's with all these birds?"

More crows had been gathering on the stairs, and they were starting to make a real racket.

Rachel slowly turned around. "What's that smell?"

Under an overhanging branch on the sidewalk by the stairs, two dead raccoons lay on their sides.

Stephanie came up behind her. "How about we go back?"

"Good idea." As they were retreating, three crows flew down to the door, forcing the girls to the side wall. "We may have to climb over."

Two more crows set down on the corners of the wall. "Think of something!"

Suddenly, the bronze doors burst open and four guys came out of the building.

The birds flew off.

"David!"

"Rachel?" He stopped in mid-stride. "What are you doing here? Waiting for Mark and Larry?"

Shaking, she said, ". . .They're on the trip to the stock exchange. Uh. . . . We were talking to someone. Are you and your buddies going to the dorm? Can we join ya?"

"You don't need an invitation." David waved them on and smiled at his friends.

Going down the steps, a stocky guy in front said, "Check out the dead raccoons. What are they doing here? I don't recall seeing them earlier. Probably why the birds. . . ."

The girls rolled their eyes at each other.

In the dorm hallway, Rachel pointed to their door. "That large package must be from my brothers, but I don't know about the smaller one." She bent down at the knees. "It says *To Mark Lexington*. Wow. I wonder who brought it here."

"Don't know." Stephanie unlocked the door and turned on the light. "Those birds freaked me *out*." She booted up her computer.

Rachel threw the boxes onto her bed and broke the seals with her keys. "Me, too. Thank God for David and his friends." She opened the larger box and found a rope and a note.

Stephanie pulled up the shades near the machine. "You think they were trained birds?"

Rachel, who'd slipped the coiled rope over her shoulder, was too busy reading the note to respond.

*Welcome. You got mail,* the computer announced.

Stephanie clicked the e-mail icon and found a message from her

father. "Rachel, my dad is bringing his friend to the awards dinner
. . . . Did ya hear?" Stephanie turned to Rachel and turned white.

Rachel asked, "What's wrong?"

"Seeing you with that rope around your shoulders proves
there's no turning back."

# CHAPTER 17

WHEN THEY COULDN'T OPEN the library windows at 11:00 Saturday night, Stephanie shook her flashlight. "Forget the tunnels. Why don't we try the front door of the church?"

Rachel nodded, looking thoughtfully at the overcast, windy sky. "Why not? Father Murray's cool."

Minutes later, Mark was turning the knob of the eleven-foot oak door to the gothic building. It squeaked open. "We're in." He eased the door shut. The only light came from a few flickering candles on the window sills.

"What in God's name are *you* four doing here?" The voice had come from the open doorway leading to the main aisle.

"Father Murray!" Rachel shone a beam of light at his shoes. "Hi."

"Hello." The white-haired rector, a man of medium build, crossed his arms. "What's with the rope, Mark? And, Rachel, why do you have a flashlight? . . . You're here for the documents!" He had noticed the tool box in Larry's hands and sighed. ". . . Well, I suppose it can't be helped. I've seen enough to—go that way." He indicated to a circular staircase in the corner behind them. "Please be careful. I'll cover for you."

Rachel hugged him. "Thanks, Father."

When they were out of his sight, he made the sign of the cross.

A little later, Mark lifted the trap door on the southwest corner of the belfry and ran his flashlight around the room. "This is it."

The setup and continuous movement of machinery kept them silent. The smell of oil made them sniffle.

Stephanie coughed. "God, what a lot of dust!"

Mark saw Rachel move to the western face of the clock. "Careful, everyone."

Larry directed his light on the southern face. "There's glass on each dial, to keep the dust out."

Mark said, "I'm gonna put this rope in the far corner under the ladder. Rach, Steph, you better put your hair up."

They did as Mark said and gathered around the south face, which looked out on the campus.

Stephanie swung the flashlight beam in a circle. "Didn't realize how *large* these clocks are."

Mark asked, "How big do you figure? Ten, twelve feet?"

"Fifteen," said Rachel. "That's according to the Internet."

Mark directed the light at a maze of support beams.

Larry turned to him. "The motor sounds like. . . ."

"It's loud."

Rachel pointed. "That black oval thing. . .that's the cast-iron carriage that holds the motor. See the platform?" She moved the beam along the floor. "That large wheel, and the smaller one near the clock, are the hour and minute wheels. They're connected by rods. And the small wheel that looks like a pound sign is a pinion. Turns the wheels. Bet you can get a nasty cut from those edges."

The guys stared at her. "Someone's been doing her homework."

"This constant motion can make you dizzy," said Stephanie.

Larry shook his flashlight. "Look at the size of those teeth in the gears. Like a shark's."

Rachel pulled out the document the ghost had given her. "This says 'Winding mechanism. North.'" She pointed. "That's the long, narrow rod connected to the drum of this main wheel." She spotlighted the device that stuck out furthest from the mechanism and turned to the others. "What are we waiting for?"

With Mark in the lead, they crossed the room on a frame of two-by-fours, edging their way around vertical beams.

At the north face, just as Rachel was about to speak, the bell sounded.

"What was that?"

Mark put up his flashlight to his watch. "Relax. It's eleven-thirty."

Stephanie shivered. "It's colder here, but not as dark."

The guys looked at each other. "Don't tell me there's a ghostly presence," Mark murmured.

"He's helping us." Rachel waved the flashlight above, below, and alongside the device.

Stephanie began to tap the floor. "You really think this professor put paperwork in there?"

"We'll soon find out." Rachel held out a hand to Larry. "Can I have a screwdriver?"

During an argument between Rachel and Mark about who was going to retrieve the lost papers, Stephanie remained quiet, but

Larry shouted, "I'll do it!" He grabbed a screwdriver from the tool-box. "Shine the light from above, Steph." He slipped the tool underneath the lip of the small knob from one side and pulled it toward him. He did that all around, four times, until he could unscrew the piece with his hand. The brass knob fell off onto the wood.

Rachel stepped on it.

Stephanie aimed the flashlight into the rod. Her mouth fell open.

"What is it?" Rachel shone the light on Stephanie's motionless face.

"There's. . .*paper* inside."

Larry was already jiggling the tools in the box. He came up with a long tweezers. Grabbing his wrist to stop his arm from shaking, he slid the instrument into the narrow cylinder. Moments later, he extracted a rolled-up sheet of yellow paper. They were silent, but the machinery kept clunking along.

Mark unrolled it and smiled. *Origins of Knights University, by Gordon Cunningham.* "Wow." He broke the silence and shone the light on the roof. "That was simple. Now we have to see what's in the railing."

Larry tapped the knob back onto the winding mechanism.

Below the metal ladder, Mark asked Rachel, "Ready?" He lifted her up at the waist with the flashlight snug in her mouth until she could grab the first rung.

Larry did the same with Stephanie but had to give her a boost under her rear end.

Once Mark pulled in the rope for the tool box, Larry climbed up.

"Rachel." Mark gathered them together. They were in the much smaller open section above the bells and below the hexagonal roof and weathervane. "The wind and the clouds have gotten worse. Maybe I should go up there."

"No." Rachel shook her head. "It would be easier for the three of you to support me."

Looking at the others, Mark frowned. "Okay. But be careful."

She again pulled the sheet of paper from her pocket. "It says 'NW railing.'" She pointed in the direction of the cemetery. "Here's the game plan. I'll get up on the ledge and throw the rope around the weathervane. You guys'll be holding me. When it's secure, one of you hold the other end in here. I'll climb up and dig for the other documents."

When they gasped, she flipped her hand. "Relax. I used to climb with friends to the top of the rollercoaster at Seaside during the winter."

Stephanie asked, "Is there anything you *haven't* done?"

"Never been to an air show."

Larry began digging through the toolbox for a wrench, hammer, and pliers.

Mark put the rope around Rachel's shoulder. "Watch yourself."

Stephanie asked, "What was that flash?" She looked at the dorms.

No one moved. They heard thunder in the distance.

When Rachel reached the iron railing, the wind blew her hair against her face. She slipped the tools under her belt.

"Ready?"

She nodded, grabbed an iron post, and climbed up one foot at a time. Then she switched hands and turned around.

The three held her ankles and knees.

Gently, Rachel slid the rope along her neck until she had it in her right hand. With a grunt she swung the rope but missed the bird-shaped weathervane.

On the third attempt, the rope went around it.

Larry snatched one end; Rachel grabbed the other with both hands.

That's when Stephanie began to scream.

Rachel yelled, "What the hell is going on in there?"

Larry shouted, "Stephanie, what's wrong?"

With a screwdriver, Stephanie was charging two crows at the other end. "Get *outta* here!"

"Stephanie!"

She dropped the tool and took deep breaths. "Sorry. But after yesterday...."

Looking up, Mark whispered, "Everything's fine. Keep going."

Moments later, Rachel was out of sight. When she had her foot on the north railing, she saw a lightning bolt in the west and heard thunder louder than before. She grabbed the hammer from behind her and started pounding at the enclosed gutter. It vibrated. A blast of wind swung the metal birds on the apex of the roof.

Rachel took a couple of deep breaths and began to pound again. A part of the gutter cracked. Before pounding, she had noticed a split that ran the length of the piece. She pounded some more, breaking it in two. Then she saw something that wasn't part of the railing. She replaced the hammer and grabbed the pliers to pull the thin rusted cylinder onto another piece of the gutter. "Cool." She knocked on the roof three times. A gust of wind caught her hair, and she covered the cylinder with her hand.

They looked up. "She found something!" Mark gasped.

Pulling out the wrench, she transferred the cylinder to it. Suddenly, she turned to the weathervane and screamed.

A large crow was staring at her.

The pliers went flying out of her hand. "Shit!"

"What was that?" Stephanie asked.

With her other hand on the wrench, Rachel spit at the bird. It flew off. She lowered her head and took a deep breath. Using the wrench, she put the cylinder under her belt loops and fastened it with the plastic clips that were in her pocket.

Lightning lit up the sky, and thunder shook her.

Rachel knocked twice on the roof.

Mark said, "She's ready to come back."

A gust of wind blew hair in her face, but she started to climb down. She felt drops of rain. "Not now. Christ!" The skies opened.

Mark gulped, "It's starting to pour!"

Rachel began to lose her grip on the rope as her feet slide down the roof and over the railing. "No!"

The tension on the rope forced Larry to bend at the knees.

The weathervane started to squeal and lean to one side.

"*Rachel*!" Mark reached out for her but missed when the wind shifted horizontally, driving her body away from the roof.

She screamed, "Mark!" as she slipped further below the opening.

Another shift in the wind shoved her body back toward the railing.

"Steph, hold my belt!" Leaning downward, Mark grabbed Rachel's waist. "I gotcha! Climb up!" he shouted.

She did and leaned onto Mark, who fell back and bumped Stephanie out of the way. He got a mouthful of wet rope.

Larry let go of his end of the rope and stumbled backward but stayed on his feet. He and Stephanie helped the two up.

Hugging Rachel, Mark said, "You're soaked, you crazy broad." Then he saw the container on her belt. "You got it."

"Yes." She stared into his eyes.

At the railing, Larry pulled up the remaining rope.

"How did the professor get them *up* there?" Stephanie wondered.

Rachel noticed scrapes on her hands. "Fear and desperation are powerful motivators."

Rope coiled around his shoulder, Larry said, "Time to leave."

Thunder sent them climbing down the ladder.

In the chancel, they found the priest. "Father!" Rachel yelped.

"Drop this?" He held up the pliers and gave them to her. "Rachel, my dear, you're disheveled." He approached. "Did you find what you were looking for?"

"Yes."

"Follow me." He led them past the sputtering candles and through a small conference room to a back door. On the way, he plucked a towel off a chair. He unlocked the door and turned on a light above the stairs.

On the basement floor, Rachel whispered, "Father, you know about the tunnels?"

He lifted his hands. "I believe in God, Father Almighty, creator of Heaven and Earth, and Jesus Christ his only son, but demons from Hell run this school. What you found will bring peace and justice to this university. I'm too old to do it myself, but if I can help. . . ." He draped the towel around Rachel's shoulders. "Take this." He gave her a key. "Go to your right. Fifty feet down, the passageway splits three ways. Take the middle tunnel. It'll lead you to your dorm."

# CHAPTER 18

A FTER DINNER ON SUNDAY NIGHT, the four conspirators were sitting on the floor, their backs against the beds of the men's dorm room. In the light of two gooseneck lamps, shades down, with music coming from the radio on Mark's desk, they were shuffling through and reading what they'd found.

Rachel read the back of the picture she was holding: "Monks take break from repairing steps, 1964." She grunted. "Those are the stairs we took when we were in the tunnels."

Whispering, Mark said, "Here's a picture from 1963 of the torture chamber where we crossed paths with that monk last month."

Rachel nudged him on the arm. "And here's one of what looks like a weapons closet. I think I can make out some black crows in cages."

Stephanie positioned a black-and-white photo directly under the light. "This shot reminds me of the Knights of the Round Table."

"Look!" Larry said. "Rows and rows of wine bottles stacked along the walls. Judging from the suits worn by these two guys next to the monks, I'd say this was during Prohibition. I can't make out the names of the back, but here's *Gambino family. 1927.*"

"On the back of the one I'm holding—" Rachel turned it around— "it says, *Supply Room of Knights Hall, 1938.*"

Stephanie nodded. "These must be the rooms behind those other doors next to the torture chamber."

"This blows me away," said Mark, flipping another photo. "Here's a stocky guy with two monks in the old library. On the lower right, it says: *Phil Fontanata at Knights U. 2/19/1947.*" He put that down on his lap, picked up an article from the *Daily News*, and read, "'Reputed mobster Phil Fontanata of the Gambino family has been on the run since he shot a New York Court of Appeals judge twice in the head. Judge'—I can't pronounce his Greek name—'was an honest man who could not be bought.' Blah blah blah. . . . 'Mr. Fontanata was last seen near Suffern, New York. Five feet, nine inches tall and weighing two hundred twenty pounds, he has dark hair, brown eyes, a thick nose, and a scar above his right eye. He is considered armed and dangerous.'"

"Rachel." Larry nodded. "So the story you told about the Mafia was also on the money."

"Yep." Rachel studied an architect's rendering. "This is a blueprint of the campus." She traced her finger near the edge of it. "It shows a tunnel from Memorial Hall to Knights. That's how they kidnapped Mel. But it doesn't show Welch Hall."

"Welch wasn't built until 1970," Mark said. "I noticed the last page of the document was dated 1965."

"More Mafia involvement." Larry held up four different items clipped together. "A bank deposit indicating fifty thousand dollars deposited in cash in 1961. Savings account number 281-something.

The name of the bank, and the date, are missing. On the memo line, 'Knights University.'" He switched to a regular sheet. "Supposedly this is a fifty-thousand dollar donation from the Temple family. But it's really drug money from the Gambinos. The following day, the money was turned into checks, one for twenty thousand made payable to a school scholarship fund. The other, for thirty thousand, went to the wife of a Gambino soldier. It's signed *G. Cunningham.*" He held up another sheet of paper with a old copy of two checks. "The ink on the woman's maiden name is blurred . . .Pam something. And lastly, a *New York Post* article, dated March 5, 1961, has the headline '$50,000 Worth of Heroin Hits the South Bronx.'"

"Money laundering," Mark concluded.

Rachel grinned at him. "President O'Connor did say more goes on at this school then murder and kidnapping."

"It doesn't end." Stephanie shook her head. "Here's an article from *University Times.* 'Professor Teddy Emerson found dead in his nearby house. He died of a heart attack.'" She looked at the bottom of it. "In blue letters, G. Cunningham wrote: '*Scared to death in torture chamber.*'" She flipped to a second sheet taped to the newspaper piece. "'*I, Professor Ted Emerson, admit to participating in a human sacrifice on a mere child who held opposing views of this college. This nineteen-year-old boy came to Knights U. to major in sociology. Never in my worst nightmares could I have foreseen that a student who favored socialism would end up shooting himself after hours of torture. He was nearly clubbed to death, whipped, and tied to a long two-by-four on which we lowered his head into a bucket of water. He had no real choice—either shoot himself and leave a suicide note, or extend the pain. If he re-*

fused the gun, the other Knights had decided to place him in the iron maiden. On the suicide note, he was forced to write he couldn't handle the pressure of college life anymore. Since he had no energy left, one of the monks helped him pull the trigger. Also, I regret to admit putting local police on the university payroll. Signed, Teddy Emerson.'" Stephanie dropped the papers. "Sergeant Dolan. That explains the roadblocks and excuses surrounding the last two disappearances."

"Another college suicide? Happens all the time, huh?" Rachel sighed. "I have a private memo from Dean Temple to the administration, summer 1960. It's a list of courses under consideration by Knights U. for the fall semester. 'Acceptable: Renaissance Art, American History, American Nineteenth-Century Literature, Principles of Conservatism, The Free Market, The Philosophies of Aristotle,' and so on. 'Unacceptable: The Liberal Movement, The Rise of Communism, Intro to Eastern Philosophy, The Articles of Confederation,' and so on. 'Signed, Joe Temple III.'" She glanced at Stephanie. "Steph, you read well out loud. What did Professor Cunningham write before he was killed?"

Stephanie picked up the four page document and cleared her throat:

*Origins of Knights University*
*by History Professor Gordon Cunningham, Ph.D.*

*Ten former Harvard professors, led by Edward Knights and Joe Temple, along with Davis, Loyal, Bishop, Clark, Welch, Marshall, York, and Reddington, founded a university in Rockland County, New York. They wanted to educate socially connected, right-wing, young white males in the disciplines of capitalism, Western philosophy, art, literature, and American history to carry on the traditions established in the U.S. Constitution by such articulate men as George Washington, Thomas Jefferson, John Adams, Benjamin Franklin, Alexander Hamilton, and other Founding Fathers. To protect and maintain the objectives of this university, these men, fanatic followers of Freemasons, Knights Templar, and The Rosicrucians, decided to create the Knights of the Temple as defense against anyone who opposed their beliefs. The Gambino family helps finance the school.*

*At Harvard University in 1900, the president of the school had abolished all requirements for undergraduates. The student body was specializing in nothing and mainly taking introductory courses. Professor Edward Knights, who was raised in the Midwest and whose grandfather was a Freemason and fought as a Union officer in the Civil War, did not approve of this unstructured system. He felt ideas from other cultures, contrary to the thoughts and practices of Western European males, could seep into the university. He was not alone. Another Midwesterner, Professor Joe Temple, and eight other instructors from various parts of the nation had Freemason relatives who had fought the British, Indians, and the Confederacy, and believed the same thing.*

*For months, south of the college in a log cabin, these ten had secret meetings about how the school should be run. On the subject of capitalism, they saw its beauty translated into the Industrial Revolution, which was building America into a political and economic powerhouse. Socialism, they felt, pulled the economy apart. They saw how Socrates, Aristotle, and Plato had influenced others, like Franklin, and Hamilton, to create a document that solidified a nation. They themselves had encountered the savagery of Indians, and they argued that, if the White men hadn't forced the Red men off the land, there wouldn't be a United States. Crossing the path of the Black men, the ten had found them unfriendly and concluded that White men ought to dominate. In time, they felt it was time to act.*

Stephanie asked, "Larry, can you please get me a drink of water?"

*One chilly March night in Harvard yard, these professors, led by Edward Knights, carried torches and a list of courses and standards they wanted established at Harvard to the administration. The Civil War had taught them the importance of union, and Harvard, like other colleges, had failed to deliver. The school officials immediately halted this protest and expelled the radicals from the university.*

*While in exile, these men read the Constitution*

*and the Declaration of Independence over and over, until they knew them by heart. Practices, beliefs, and ideas of Freemasons, Knights Templar, and the Rosicrucians became second nature to them. They taught themselves everything there was to know about capitalism.*

*Edward Knights was a leader and an advocate for national rights; at a Freemason meeting, prior to the rally, a senior member had shown him a copy of a document called "The Protocols of the Wise Men of Zion." Its exact origin is unclear, but the report was a piece on world domination. The paper changed his life forever: That night he heard his brother's family had been savagely murdered by immigrants two weeks before.*

*When they heard rumors from Albany that the thirtieth-fourth governor, Benjamin B.O. Dell, Jr. 1901-1904, and his family wanted to start a college in lower New York, they thought of founding their own university, consisting of the subjects they'd been studying; it would be their chance to correct on a small scale the direction America was taking.*

Larry handed Stephanie the glass of water. "Thanks," she said, gratefully raised the class of water to her lips, and took a long swallow.

*In New York City, they crossed paths with a Mario Costello, whose Brooklyn-based family was associated with an organization that would in time become the Gambino group. Since Costello liked the project, he and his associates decided to help finance the school and change the professors' appearances. In trouble with the law from age six, the tall and stocky Costello brought his new friends to Brooklyn. He suggested calling the new college "Knights University," since Edward Knights was the driving force behind it. Costello was happy to hear that Knights and the others wanted to build tunnels under the school in order to exercise control.*

*Decades later, a Mafia fugitive used the tunnels when he was sought by the FBI for murdering a New York Court of Appeals judge. He hid at the school for weeks before the search for him lost steam. The school warehoused alcohol during prohibition. Once the Mafia began dealing drugs, KU laundered the dirty money into New York and New Jersey banks.*

Stephanie coughed.

*Before ground broke on the university, Costello and his associates kidnapped the governor's nephew at gunpoint. They told him one version of the story: "You founded Knights University. You'll get an academic building and dormitory named after you, Freemun and Jon's Hall. However, these professors determine the guidelines of the school. You thought*

Knights was a perfect name for a college, since knights are constantly learning new skills."

My involvement in Knights University began in 1956 when my wife and I moved to Pearl River, New York, since her parents had become sick and needed assistance. I was accepted into the small but growing school with open arms. The administration, and my fellow professors, were impressed with my credentials as a former Harvard history professor. It did not take long for me to notice strange things on campus: an all-White male student body more typical of the South, and courses that consisted of Aristotle, Milton, Darwinism, the free-enterprise system, and little else.

After one of the faculty, a Professor Emerson, disappeared one night, my life changed. That's when I was introduced to the Knights of the Temple, who rivaled the Assassins, who were active during biblical times. K & T identified themselves with the letters burnt on their wrists. K & T thought I had what it took to defend the principles of the school with my life. When I saw the tunnels, the torture chamber where people were jailed, dumped in burning oil, and lost limbs for disagreeing with my colleagues, I knew I had to do something. This document is that something. For almost nine years, I've been researching it. These criminals blamed the KKK for hanging that Black boy last year.

"Go to the police," my wife tells me. She

*doesn't understand my colleagues' power and influence. I'm not strong but scared as hell. They're on to me, since I've spoken to former Knights' professors, read about the rebellion, and researched the Harvard connection. Along with this report, there are signed statements and confessions, newspaper clippings, and photographs. I'm not a survival-of-the-fittest type as Darwin preaches. That's what these people have grown to believe, which has led to secularism as their belief system. The only faith I have remaining is that someone will someday find these papers and expose this university to the world. As I type these last few words, I would like to express how much I love my wife and kids. God help them, me, and the good people of this university.*

*—G.I.C*
*May 8, 1965*

Stephanie laid down the document. Except for a commercial on the radio, the room was quiet. Mark pointed to the carpet. "What's that?"

Picking up a single sheet of paper, Larry said, "Form from the admission package."

"There's something written on the back."

Larry flipped the sheet halfway. "'Build character. Challenge yourself. Prepare for the future at Knights University. Over sixty years of proven education and tradition. Major in disciplines like communications, political science, American History, and more.

Make Knights U. your home for your undergraduate and graduate studies.'" He shook his head. "There's pictures of Knights Hall, the Marshall Complex, and Nicky's Field. There's also a photo of students traveling to class. 'Knights University in Suffern, New York, Rockland County, is approximately forty minutes northwest of New York City, the financial, communication, and advertising capital of the world.'"

He turned over the sheet. "'Returning from one of our secret K & T meetings, Oscar and I went to his office in the admissions department to continue a prior conversation. He was extremely upbeat, since previously he had sent a rejection letter to a young man whose SAT scores were low in English and he would have required financial aid. Oscar was so excited, he took notes during the session at the round table. Normally, only the headmaster did so. Before I left, I lied about needing a phone number, and he wrote it on this. Here's a sample of what was said on April 22, 1964.'" Larry took a deep breath. "'Unless you're a rich White male, with family connected to upper government or big business, and the mind-set of a federalist and capitalist, unless you adhere to western philosophical thought and are non-religious, don't bother applying here. We must keep America politically, economically, and socially strong; otherwise it'll fall like the Roman Empire. Capitalism, democracy to a point, and the English language are the USA. *Oscar York III.*'"

Larry dropped the sheet where he found it. "Now what?"

Stephanie moved her legs to sit Indian style. "Make copies. I'll send 'em to my father."

Rachel snapped her fingers. "Research that guy Fontanata at the library. Money laundering!"

Mark sighed. "Have the freshmen bring 'em to the *Times*."

Picking up the form, glancing at both sides as if she was about to throw up, Rachel said, "Talk about a hidden agenda."

# CHAPTER 19

RACHEL WAS IN THE CAFETERIA on Monday, a forkful of salad in front of her mouth, when she realized that the Tree and Fatso were looking at the picture of the torture chamber on the corner of the table. "What are you two doing?"

"Is that your playroom?"

Rachel kept eating. "It's my basement in Toms River."

The girls stepped back.

Rachel nodded. "My brothers found it on Ebay. They bought two photos and sent me one. Years ago we'd tell ghost stories. Like about this old TV repairman who collected dishwashers, ovens, vacuum cleaners, and turned them into killing machines. And other strange happenings in haunted houses along the shore. And this was one of 'em."

Theresa, thin nose prominent in her long face, said, "Careful, Mark. She probably uses it on her ex-boyfriends. And we know she's had plenty."

Rachel jumped up. "You don't know what you're—" Mark grabbed her. "I'm going to put a curse on both of you that'll knock you out. I'll stuff you in my trunk, take you down there, and put you through each machine."

They marched off.

Stephanie said, "You sound like the monks."

"Think they'll open their big mouths?"

Mark shook ketchup on his fries. "Your reputation as a witch will flourish!"

Rachel sat up. "I can live with that."

"Learn anything?"

"Like what?"

Larry finished his burger. "Like be careful with that stuff?"

Rachel turned over the picture. "Let's just hope we don't end up there."

Later on, Rachel was making copies of her term paper outside the reference room when, staring at a framed portrait of Rembrandt, she wondered if *he* had been a member of a secret society.

Someone tapped her on the shoulder, and she screamed. "You almost gave me a heart attack!"

"Sorry." Heglan shrugged. "What're you doing?"

She pushed black strands of her hair out of her face. "What does it *look* like I'm doing? Making copies of my final paper."

Heglan leaned toward the tray. "What's it on?"

"Secret societies."

He nodded. "You don't believe in them, do you?"

"Anything's possible."

He stroked his mustache. "You going to the Awards Dinner?"

She smiled. "I already have a date."

"Really?"

The copier began to make a noise. When she saw the number

of pages flashing, she asked, "Can you get me more paper?"

He went to the corner table to unlock a cabinet and gave her a ream.

Ripping it open, she said, "With Mark Lexington. The tall, good-looking guy with broad shoulders and a goatee?" She put paper in the machine. "He's also a deejay."

He asked, "Any plans after graduation? Graduate school?"

She nodded. "The four of us have been accepted at Rutgers. Also, we'll be interning at a new radio station in South Jersey."

He said, "Libraries can always use help."

"Thanks." Hand on the machine, Rachel crossed one foot over the other. "Has this place always been named Schmidt?"

"No. Cunningham. . . . But we're not supposed to mention that name!"

"Why not?"

The man's expression grew angry. "He was fired over a suspicion of embezzlement. His in-laws were sick, and he needed money. Mr. Cunningham also helped some undesirables!"

"Undesirables?"

"Students who should have failed. He fixed their grades. And he was like a Benedict Arnold!" He punched the machine. "Forget it! I'm going to be a chaperone for the Yankees game during senior week, and I noticed your name on the list."

"David!" She stepped away from the copier, watching the pudgy librarian stomp back to the front desk. "How ya doing?"

The guy, who had a two-days' growth on his face, shrugged. "What's up, Rachel? Why was he yelling?"

"Don't worry about it. Last minute work?"

"Yep." He lowered his voice. "You got Mark's package, right?"

She raised her eyebrows. "You're the one who brought it over?"

He nodded. "I figured it was important. Weird shit goes on at this school. . . ."

"You can say that again. Where you off to?"

"Nonfiction." He pointed to the rear of the building. "Catch ya later."

"Bye." She picked up the originals and two sets of copies. "Steph," she called out. "I'm done."

"Great." Stephanie had come around the corner. "I have a table set up with goodies." She coughed. "Were you involved in that outburst before?"

"Who, me?" Rachel smiled.

On a table below a wood-and-metal chandelier lay a Mafia reference book and a few economics texts. Flipping pages, Rachel stopped when she came to the headline *Gambino Family*. She skipped around the article. "'The Gambino family—the most powerful of the five crime families of New York City—first comes to prominence in the 1920s. Carlo Gambino was the inspiration for Vito Corlene of *The Godfather*.'" She kept flipping. "Oh my. Phil Fontanata." She looked up at Stephanie, encyclopedias and the windows beyond showcasing another sunny afternoon. "'Phil Fontanata was a hit man for the Gambinos,'" she said, glancing back at the page. "'Killed at least twenty people, including a New York judge. . .spent most of his time in Queens and Brooklyn. Also involved in protecting the family's gambling racket. It was rumored he took too large a percentage over the course of two years. One day he left his Queens apartment and never returned. His body was never found. They claim he's buried somewhere underneath the Coney Island boardwalk.'"

Stephanie whispered, "To think the school babysat that guy."

Rachel nodded. "The disappearance reminds me of a story my father told my brothers and me. You may not remember, but he represents developers. One builder leveled a run-down motel and a used-car lot to construct a hotel on Route 35 in Toms River. As they were clearing the land behind the motel, the workers found a skeleton. Turned out to be the body of a mobster from the Genovese family who left his house one day and never came back."

Stephanie sighed. "Money laundering is confusing. You get it illegally from one place, deposit it in a bank or something, transfer it somewhere else. . .to me, it was always when my mom washed my clothes and found a dollar bill in the pocket."

Rachel laughed. "Same thing with me."

Stephanie motioned to the computers. "I discovered Emerson was a Yale graduate who donated tons of money there. He was at the top of his class and taught Western Philosophy."

Rachel tapped her rings on the table. "Did you know this library was named after Cunningham?"

"No."

"Our pudgy friend said they're not allowed to mention his name." Her stomach growled.

"Hungry?"

They returned the books and left.

On their way to the Marshall Complex for a rock concert at Shields Bar, hand in hand with the guys, Stephanie grumbled, "Those birds are following us."

Larry swung her arm. "Don't be ridiculous."

The birds flew east toward Knights Hall.

When the four entered the building, they found a line of students showing their IDs to get in. Techno music was making the walls shake. A large copper shield with *Knights* branded into the center hung to the left of the door. *Shields Bar*, in gray, hung above it. On the right, a poster read: *Cover Band Week, sponsored by WKHU.*

The lineman-sized bouncer said, "Yo! It's the deejays."

Mark gave the guy a high-five.

Rachel pointed. "There's room by the bar." They gathered by a TV monitor, surrounded by smoke. A Mets game was on.

"Four Buds." They clicked bottles and drank. Motioning with his beer, Mark said to Rachel, "Look who's here."

She brought Stephanie with her. "Professor Drake. What brings you to Shields?"

Smoking a cigarette, the tall man replied, "I'm here to see David play. I don't drink."

Rachel took a sip. "I'd like you to meet my friend and roommate, Stephanie Brooks."

They shook hands. "Hello. Rachel, you sounded nervous yesterday on the radio like you'd found a dead body or the documents from King Solomon's Temple."

"It. . .uh, finally hit me yesterday—only two more weeks of school."

He nodded. "If I was you, I'd be careful."

"Why?"

He bent down. "There's a rumor going around about you torturing people with spells and poisons."

She gave him a wide-eyed look. "Not a word of truth in it. Pay it no mind." She laughed. "We must be getting back to the guys.

Enjoy the show. Bye."

"Nice meeting you," he said to Stephanie.

"That was weird," Stephanie whispered as they set off. Once they rejoined the guys, the blasting music stopped and the bartender announced, "Ladies and gentlemen, Knights University and WKHU are proud to present Cover Band Week. For tonight, we have The Unforgettable Fire!"

The crowd cheered. Lights over the stage fell on four guys performing "Mysterious Ways."

Rachel shrugged, seeing the Tree and Fatso near David, who was playing bass.

A couple of songs into the set, Stephanie got elbowed in the back. When she turned around to see who it was, she thought for a second she saw a figure in a white mask, but it quickly disappeared. Drake had moved to the rear of the room. During "Sunday Bloody Sunday," Stephanie glanced up at the monitor to see a masked ball with hundreds of dancing people dressed in early European outfits. As the camera zeroed in on a stunning black-haired woman in a red gown, her partner dipped her backwards. But when the audience saw a mirror in the background, there was only the lone woman's image. Stephanie asked the bartender, "What's that movie?"

He said, "Someone switched channels. *Van Helsing*, with Hugh Jackman and Kate Beckinsale."

Larry slipped his arm around her waist. "Enjoying?"

She cheered like the rest of them.

After the finale, Rachel tried to get David's attention, but the Tree and Fatso were with him. She said, "We'll see him tomorrow."

In the women's dorm, with Rachel asleep, a yawning Stephanie entered *Van Helsing*, the doctor who'd killed Dracula, on her computer. Head dropping and suddenly rising, eyelids closing and opening, clicking search, she saw the reflection of a monk suddenly dart across the screen. She leaped out of her chair and began struggling with the intruder. Before her glasses popped off, Stephanie saw two monks carry Rachel out the room. Another grabbed her from behind, covering her mouth with a handkerchief until she passed out and fell into their arms.

Minutes later, Stephanie awoke on her back, wrists and ankles bound to a stretcher. A bandanna was tied around her mouth. She began to moan.

The master patted her forehead. "There's no point in trying to escape. Soon you'll be in five parts." He laughed. "I must commend your group for finding the documents. But did you really think you were going to get away with it?" He lifted up the back of her head. "Before you're torn apart, look around the chamber."

Yellow candles lit the room. To Stephanie's left, Rachel, stripped naked, had her wrists in the blocks of the chains, feet dangling above the floor. Two monks were hitting her with a belt and a paddle. They had already broken her nose, and her lips had swelled like a clown's.

Stephanie heard screams to her right. Mark was getting lowered into a pot of boiling oil. Inhuman noises were coming from the jail.

The monk explained, "We gave Larry a new formula we were working on for aggressive behavior. It seems to have changed him." He nodded.

Another monk activated the stretcher.

Stephanie began to scream. She pushed the keyboard and

mouse off the desk and knocked over the chair. When Rachel tackled her onto the bed, she slowly quieted down. Minutes later, Rachel rolled off her onto her back, arm over her face.

Someone was pounding on the door, shouting. "Is everything all right in there?"

Rachel staggered over. "We're fine. Thank you. Everything's better. You can go back to bed." After she laid a blanket over Stephanie, Rachel fell into bed herself. She was asleep before her head hit the pillow.

# CHAPTER 20

THE FOLLOWING TUESDAY AFTERNOON was sunny but windy. Mark and Larry were the last ones off the bus near the Marshall Complex, returning from Bear Mountain. "Boy," Mark said, "those lakes were beautiful."

"Peaceful," Larry agreed.

The bus driver made a U-turn down Knights Road.

Heading toward the dorms, they saw the Tree and Fatso in the distance. Both had stains on their backs.

Mark started laughing.

Larry asked, "What's the joke?"

Mark chuckled, "When the two of them slid down the hill into that mud pit. . .thank God Rachel wasn't there, because she would've said something."

Cheers rose from the tennis courts. A Greyhound bus with New York license plates was parked along the curb.

Mark said, "Theresa will never forgive Rachel for becoming captain of the soccer and basketball teams."

Larry nodded. "And she knows that, if Rachel had played softball this year, she'd have beaten her out for captain there too again."

"Remember last year?" Mark adjusted his sunglasses. "Rachel, Steph, and Theresa were competing for two time-slots at the station?"

"Remind me."

Glancing at the church, Mark said, "Last semester there was this huge party Friday night at Swords Hall. Columbus Day celebration. Loads of people. You and Steph'd left for the weekend. Rachel and Theresa each had too much to drink. They started calling each other names. . .slut this, bitch that. At one point, Rachel needed a refill and turned her back on Theresa. So Theresa rips her sleeve, and she screamed louder than the music. And you know her. Rachel doesn't fight like a girl. She knocked Theresa out cold, nearly broke her nose, gave her a black eye."

"Whoo." Larry shook his head. "It also pisses them off that Rachel barely studies but gets an 'A' in most of her classes."

"Well, Rachel's a big reader. Science fiction, politics, true crime. I'll stick with Ludlum."

Larry snickered. "Sci-fi? True crime? Steph loves romances."

At the door to the dorm, Mark fumbled for his keys. "Both those girls are from Brooklyn, and they love to bust Rachel about New Jersey."

Larry had found his own keys and unlocked it. "I'm also from Brooklyn, and believe me, it's not Beverly Hills."

"Neither is Queens." Before he went up the stairs, Mark asked, "Those two dating anybody on campus?"

"I doubt it."

Later, at the library, the guys again saw a flock of crows in the air. Larry gasped. "Hey! That reminds me of what Stephanie said about birds following us last night. And she told me her nightmare."

Mark turned to him. "I heard about it from Rachel. It sounded scary as hell. When Stephanie thought she saw a person wearing a mask, Drake was too far back. Waiting for Saturday is rough. Think they know?"

Larry shrugged.

Up ahead, they saw Dean Sands leave Temple Hall: Mark imagined he'd been jettisoned from the mouth of the stone gargoyle over the entrance.

"Gentlemen. How are you? Where are Rachel and Stephanie?"

Mark said, "They went on a trip into Manhattan."

"That's right. I've been so busy. You two must've gone to Bear Mountain."

"Yes." Mark took a step closer. "Dean Sands, is it possible to get a recommendation from your office for the four of us? In addition to graduate school, we're applying to a new radio station in South Jersey that should go on the air in the fall. Professor Loom suggested I ask you."

"Since you spoke to Mr. Loom," Sands smiled. "I'll have my admin start the paperwork. Stop by my office and drop off the name and address of the place."

"Thanks."

"My pleasure." Sands scratched his eyebrow. "It's good to hear you're using your major. And with Knights University behind you, you're on solid ground. For decades, you know, we've been rated one of the top twenty-five colleges in the nation."

Larry crossed his arms. "Actually, *Knights U.* sounds medieval."

The man did not agree. "What? Knights stands for strength,

bravery, trust, and commitment. *You* sound like Rachel."

The guys laughed. "She does have an impact on people." It was Mark speaking.

Sands thick lips twisted into a snicker. "If it was up to her, this school would be called Jokers Wild University."

The guys laughed louder.

"In all seriousness—" the Dean squared his broad shoulders— "I'm very proud of this school. I'll do anything in my power to protect it. I can't think of a finer institution, except for my alma mater, Yale. That's why we make it difficult to be accepted here. Now, if you'll excuse me, I'm late for an appointment." He marched off.

"Excuse me, Dean Sands," Mark called out, "I'm sorry, but I'm curious about something."

The dean turned back. "What?"

"Why do you usually wear black?"

Sands took a deep breath. "Gives me a feeling of mystery. Actually, I'm partially color blind. . . . Remember, gentlemen, as Socrates said, 'Life is a contract.'" He sped off.

Mark kicked a rock. "Life's a contract? So is a pledge by a secret society. Rachel's a smart girl. You piss him off, and he says more than he should. It's also spooky how much he reminds me of Frankenstein."

Larry mumbled, "Solid ground? Top twenty-five? There are, what? Six thousand undergraduates here?"

Mark nodded. "All required to have high SAT scores. And four years of English. Three of math. Two of American history. Three of a foreign language. Two of science. Involvement in extracurricular activities. . . ."

Larry shook his head. "You'd think we'd been applying to West Point." They turned toward the Marshall Complex.

When the alley was empty, President O'Connor closed his window at Temple Hall. He sat down on a couch below a reproduction of a Da Vinci engineering diagram. Rubbing his face, he hit a prerecorded number on his cell. "Get me Gasso."

"...Yeah?"

"Peter. It's O'Connor. You and your boys better come north. Things are on edge here. My gut is telling me judgement day will happen soon."

"Keep me informed. I'll notify my superiors. If I get the green light, we should be in Suffern tomorrow."

"Thanks." O'Connor turned off the cell. "I wonder if Rachel and company went for the documents." He looked out the window at the outlines of knights on the library glass. "What are they waiting for, an audience?"

Searching for a table in the cafeteria, Mark and Larry spotted the three freshmen near the windows. "What's up, guys?"

"Hey. How you doing?"

Barbara spun a lock of her red hair. "Hello. Just the two of you? Where's Rachel and Stephanie?"

"Trip to the Museum of Television and Radio," said Mark.

Larry asked, "Can we join you?"

"Sure." Barbara pulled out the chair next to her. "Mark, you can sit here."

The seniors looked at each other. "Those chicken cutlets smell good. We'll be back." They went to the food counter.

When they returned, Larry asked, "How are finals?"

"Tough." Ralph shook his head. "For fifty minutes you write

non-stop."

Marvin cut a piece of cutlet. "Test covered everything from the first day of the semester."

Mark nodded. "They can be killers."

Barbara checked her watch. "It's almost six, and the girls aren't back yet?"

Mark laughed. "They got off to a late start because the bus had a flat tire. Typical of Rachel to be involved in something like that."

"Speaking of her," Larry cleared his throat. "When's your last day on campus?"

Barbara said, "My parents are picking me up Friday night."

"Saturday morning," Ralph and Marvin told him.

Mark leaned toward them. "We need a big favor from the three of you."

They stopped eating.

"The four of us agreed that you could handle this. We want you three to go into the city this Saturday afternoon and drop off a package at the *New York Times*."

"You got. . . ." Marvin kicked Ralph in the leg.

Mark lowered his head. "Yes. There's too much going on for us to do it. Saturday, the station's sponsoring an outdoor concert on Nicky's Field that includes food and drinks. Our families will be coming late that afternoon for the dinner."

Marvin asked, "Why are you waiting until Saturday?"

Larry said, "We know what we're doing, but the FCC will be here lecturing and recruiting the next two days."

Ralph asked, "Can you tell us how you? . . ."

The guys shook their heads. "Deal?"

The freshman nodded.

Barbara frowned. "If I were you, Mark, I'd be concerned that Rach and Steph haven't returned yet."

Mark smiled. "Nah, they're having a blast."

On the corner of Fifth Avenue and Fiftieth Street at that very moment, Stephanie was asking, "Where's the bus?"

Other buses, delivery trucks, SUVs, taxis, cars, and motorcycles were blowing their horns and releasing fumes down the avenue. Police officers were directing traffic. Suits, skirts, shoppers, tourists, other pedestrians moved north and south on both sidewalks. Crowds had built up at the corners, waiting for the light to change. Wind sent debris into the air and carried the faint aroma of diner food. The skyscrapers blocked much of the sunlight, allowing little to fall on the cathedral tower.

Rachel checked her watch. "It's five to six. We were supposed to catch the bus here at six o'clock, so don't panic."

Stephanie grumbled, "Where's everyone else?"

Rachel looked across the street at the statue of Atlas holding up a sphere between two buildings. Tourists were taking pictures of it, and a Z-100 van was parked nearby, but she saw no familiar faces. "I don't know, but if that bus doesn't show up soon, we'll head toward Rockefeller Center."

"Okay." Stephanie zipped up her pocketbook, which held the documents.

Rachel watched the light turn yellow to red. Two vehicles went straight through, and three others were in the midst of turning left onto Forty-ninth. A wall of people crossed the avenue, entertained by hip-hop from an old Nissan's stereo.

Looking around, Stephanie pointed. "There's the bus, in front of Barnes and Noble!"

They ran southward through the crowds. Near the corner, a group of tourists stopped them. "Excuse me, miss," a plump, middle-aged woman declared, arms raised, "can you take a picture of my family with Saint Patrick's in the background? We're from Iowa."

". . .Sure." Rachel regained her breath. "Smile." The family was still trying to arrange themselves. Other people were cutting in front.

"Rachel!" Stephanie yelled.

*Click.* "Here ya go." Rachel under-handed the camera to the woman. "Let's go!"

Vehicles were halfway across the intersection when Rachel and Stephanie ran across it. Horns honked at them. Zooming past Saks, Rachel felt like she was running on the soccer field. Stephanie was holding onto her glasses. Three car lengths from the corner, the light turned yellow on Forty-eighth.

"Shit!" Rachel waved Stephanie onward. "Hurry."

Their bus was idling, and the driver was looking at the side-view mirror.

As they reached the corner, the light turned green.

"*Wait!*" Both girls started waving their arms.

The automobiles began beeping at them and inching up the moment the light changed.

The girls made it onto the sidewalk, as the driver stopped the bus and opened the door.

Breathing heavily, Rachel yelled, "Professor Clark, you told us to wait for the bus up there!" She pointed at the church.

"No." Standing next to the driver, the broad-shouldered man with a mustache shook his round head. "Here. I'm sorry for the mix-up"

The other students cheered. "Rach. Steph. You guys made it. We were getting worried."

Sitting next to Rachel, Stephanie whispered, "Someone's messing with us."

# CHAPTER 21

THERESA THE TREE LOWERED HER UMBRELLA. "I didn't think it was going to stop raining." Edith, the one Rachel called "Fatso," was looking suspiciously at the still-gray sky.

"I hope it doesn't rain graduation day."

"It better not. It would ruin everything. My outfit, my hair, my shoes. . . ." Theresa stopped.

"What are you staring at?"

"The weathervane." Theresa pointed. "It's crooked. The wind wasn't blowing that hard last night."

"You're right," said Edith. "It's leaning to the left. Maybe the storm Saturday night messed it up."

"Come on." Theresa waved her on. "Let's eat."

Professor Wells, who had been walking up from Temple Hall, returned to the building after he saw the weathervane.

Up ahead, at the softball field, Rachel and Stephanie slowed down. "Hey!" said Rachel. "They were going to find out sooner or later."

Stephanie grumbled, "That's reassuring."

Rachel sped up and pulled Stephanie with her to the tennis courts. "We tell the guys and. . .wait!" She spun around.

"Now what?"

Rachel whispered, "We're going to leave *surprises* in our room."

Later on that day, along with nineteen other senior communication majors, the four conspirators were sitting near the back of a first floor lecture room in Freemun Hall, listening to an FCC representative discuss the agency's history. The presenter was using a laptop on a lab table in a space with no windows and the lights off.

Using a penlight to flip through the three-page presentation, Rachel felt something pinch her leg. She shone the light on it. It was larger than a quarter and moving fast. She brushed it off with her hand.

Stephanie whispered, "What's wrong?"

Rachel was scratching her shin. "A spider was crawling up my leg."

Stephanie said, "Bad luck to kill spiders."

Rachel shook her head.

Meanwhile, the sky had cleared. In the women's dorm with shades down and sunlight entering at the edges, a tall monk was taking the sheets off Rachel's bed. He removed the mattress cover. He lifted the mattress, looking for any slits. Once he threw it onto the floor, he examined the box spring and ran a gloved hand along the bed frame. "Shit. It's clean." Looking behind and at the back of the bed board, he shook his head. He moved his palms over the two posters. "Damn." Stepping over the bed frame, he began to search through her dresser drawers. "Last time I was here, I didn't realize how disorganized. . . ."

His short stocky partner was doing the same thing to

Stephanie's bed. "This girl is so neat, it'll take forever to make her bed just the way she had it."

The other monk laughed. "Rachel's stuff is a mess." He opened more drawers. "I tripped over another one of her shoes." He lifted a sweater from the top of the dresser. "Doesn't this girl ever dust?" He saw jewelry, loose change, hairbrushes, and a lamp. "Her mirror could use a wipe, too." Shaking his head, he turned to the closet door. As he opened it, a large black thing flew out and hit him in the mask. He stumbled back, almost tripping.

"What's wrong?"

Bending down to pick up the object, the monk grumbled, "A booby trap. This witch on a broomstick nailed me in the face."

The other monk chuckled. "Be thankful for your mask."

The tall monk threw the stick into the closet and began searching it. "Clean." He went over to Rachel's desk, covered in papers. "She's worse than the professors." He huffed. "There's tape on the drawers."

Going through Stephanie's clothes, the shorter monk nodded. "The blonde did the same thing. She also put tape on the computer's start button."

Running a hand over Rachel's books, the other said, "Ann Rule. Issac Asimov. *Turgenev*. Built and brainy. . . . I'll check the bathroom." Before he turned on the light, he looked to see if there were any wires connected to the switch. Nothing. His work boots squished on the wet towel below the sink. The counter was filled with face creams, perfume, hair spray, hand soap, and lipsticks. A plunger sat next to the toilet. When he opened the medicine cabinet, he muffled a scream. "Is that blood?" On the bottom shelf, a mask had two horizontal red lines on it above and below the eye holes. "Wait." He picked it up. "It's lipstick."

The other monk shook his head and opened Stephanie's closet door. He stepped back when he saw a black cat hanging from the pole. He took a deep breath, when he realized it was a stuffed animal.

The tall monk crossed his arms. "They must have the documents on 'em. Maybe the others will have better luck in the guys' dorm. Let's try the redheaded freshman's room."

They replaced everything and left.

Throwing the pillow against the bed board, a third monk broad-shouldered and burly, turned over Mark's chair and saw nothing. He felt near the bulb of a black goose-neck lamp next to a window with the shades down. He shook his head. Searching through the dresser drawers, he found a comb and a dollar bill. He sneezed from the dust on the back of the mirror. On his hands and knees, he felt the carpet for any openings. He opened the desk drawers, moved textbooks, flipped through paperbacks, lifted up the keyboard. "He taped the mouse. Having any luck?"

The other monk shook his head. "Larry also taped things down."

The larger monk moved the telephone, the answering machine, the radio. "I'll check the bathroom." He switched on the light; music emerged from a smaller radio on a ledge by the toilet. It made him skip a beat. His dress shoes squeaked on the tile floor. On the counter and in the medicine cabinet, he saw toothpaste, toothbrushes, shaving cream, razors. In a huff, he killed the light and the music. "I'm going to try their secret hiding place."

The other monk joined him at the closet door.

Up on his toes, holding onto the doorframe, he slid a piece of wood sideways at the edge of the shelf that been cut into it years before. Feeling with his gloved fingers, he touched a metal object. "Got something." He pulled it out. "A tool box." He gave it to his partner, who put it on the floor. He also pulled out a manila folder. "The documents. I feel something else." There was a snap. "*Ah! Fuck!*" He had a mouse trap dangling from his ring finger. "Those sons-of-bitches." He unhooked the trap and threw it into the secret place. Blood was dripping down his finger. "I'll be in the bathroom."

The other monk stomped the floor. "They didn't learn from the first time? . . .

Should we open the folder?"

"No." A voice came from the bathroom. "We have to fix up this place. It felt about the right thickness."

After fifteen minutes of cleaning, they left the room.

Later, in the torture chamber, the master shouted, "*Fools! Idiots!*" He whipped the two monks, locked in the racks, who had been searching the guys' dorm. "How could you two've been *so* stupid?"

At that moment, two other monks entered the candle-lit chamber but stopped when they saw the punishment. They moved to the stretcher.

One of them asked, "What's with the ritual?"

The master picked up a manila folder. "They thought they had the documents in their possession, but here's what they found."

The taller monk said, "I like the blonde in the white bikini."

"Gentlemen!" the master shouted. "Put that stuff back in the folder." They followed his orders. Whip in hands, he approached them. "Since you two are empty-handed, this means war! By now, they must have made copies." He gestured to the racks. "They had my hopes up. Release them." The two ran to the others. He re-joined them. "I can't believe how stupid I've been not to go up to the tower. Time is slipping away, men. Figure out a way to defeat those four!" He flung the whip away and hurried out.

In an another part of the campus, after the bell rang in a first floor classroom at Freemun Hall, a slim African-American woman employed by the FCC closed her laptop and said, "Good luck, Rachel, with your plans. It was nice meeting you." She left.

"Bye, Mrs. Spence." The last in the room, Rachel was still scribbling notes. Stephanie had gone to the bathroom.

For the afternoon, the FCC had organized smaller group sessions, consisting of five to six students each, on a variety of subjects. Rachel and Stephanie had taken a class on marketing in radio. The guys had chosen instruction on radio instrumentation held on the second floor.

Clouds again blocked the sunlight that had been pouring in on Rachel, sitting one row from the windows. Slipping the sheet into her purse, she made her way to the door. She began to rub her arms and felt a chill on her legs. When she reached the last row, the door slammed shut and the lights went off. She back-pedaled, bumping into a chair. Turning around, she saw a ghost at the front. A spirit she'd never seen before, with all its limbs attached. It was writing something on the whiteboard. She had become a statue. Without warning, it flew across the room to the open windows. The lights came on and the door opened. She sank into a chair.

"Rachel, you still. . . ." Stephanie entered the room. "What's wrong?" She ran to her. "You're white as a sheet!" She felt her forehead. "You don't have a fever."

Rachel took a deep breath. "I—I saw. . .a ghost."

"What?"

Rachel pointed to the front.

Stephanie read: "*BEWARE, T. E.*" written on the whiteboard. "T. E?" She scratched her head. "Professor Teddy Emerson." She had Rachel by the shoulders. "Can you get up?"

Rachel got to her feet and hugged Stephanie.

Outside, under a blue sky on the way to the dorm, Rachel told Stephanie about it.

"Another helpful ghost."

Rachel asked, "Where are the guys?" Her cell rang. "What's up, sweetie?" She smiled. ". . .Sounds good. . . . Really?" She nodded. "Great to hear it. Tell me about it at dinner. About half an hour." She bit her tongue. ". . .They did? . . . Love ya. Bye." She turned it off. "The guys had visitors in their dorm. And they took the bait."

Stephanie nodded. "Good idea about the booby traps."

Two black crows flew overhead.

"Not again."

"Rachel! Stephanie!" Marvin called out, approaching them from the other way. "What's up?"

They were near Loyal Hall; Rachel spun him around. "Walk us to our dorm."

He stopped. "But mine's in the other direction."

The girls put their arms around him. "Won't you do it for us?"

"Since you put it that way. . . ."

At eight P.M., with Queensryche playing on the radio in the women's dorm, Mark was tightening a screw into the doorframe above the light switch for the chain on the girl's door. His back to

Rachel, he said, "My uncle showed me how to put these on."

She said, "That should stop them from coming in here again."

"There." He stepped over. "It's secure."

She asked, "Isn't the lock too close to the door?"

He shrugged. "The package came this morning."

She kissed him. "That's great. And I forgot to thank you and Larry for getting Ralph and the others to agree to drop the documents off."

Mark put his arm around her. "You told me about the problem with the bus and Professor Clark, but I didn't get the chance to ask you. How was the trip?"

"Good." She smiled. "At the museum, we listened to radio transmissions from the Seventies. Saw old station layouts. Had lunch in Rockefeller Center, too, next to where people ice skate."

"I've never been there." He heard voices on the other side of the door.

Rachel gulped. "That must be Larry and Steph back from Shields."

The doorknob began turning, then stopped. The door began to shake.

"No! *Wait!*"

The door was shoved open, breaking part of the doorframe, sending pieces of wood and metal across the room to the shade above Rachel's computer. Mark and Rachel ducked. The fragments hit her lamp, knocking out the light.

Stephanie and Larry stood in the doorway with their hands on their mouths.

Rachel embraced Mark. "'A' for effort, sweetie."

# CHAPTER 22

ONCE THE LAST SHEET OF PAPER was handed out, an assistant director of human resources for the FCC began to explain the admission process. Rachel and the others were sitting in the middle of the room. They figured, in case the internship at the South Jersey radio station led nowhere, the FCC could be their backup. As their class dean had mentioned, the government offered great benefits.

Rachel began rubbing her arms. Oh, God, she thought, *is the ghost of Professor Emerson here?* She started looking around the room.

Stephanie leaned over. "What are you doing?"

"Nothing."

The air conditioner kicked in.

Rachel took a deep breath and felt something crawl up her leg. Shining the penlight, she saw another spider traveling up her calf. "Unbelievable," she mumbled. About to fling it off, she remembered what had happened the day before, pressed the paper against her leg for the spider to crawl onto, and lowered the creature to the floor.

Stephanie whispered, "Don't tell me—another one?"

Rachel nodded. "I bet you it was from the monks! I had to put ice on yesterday's bite."

Outside the Marshall Complex, in sixty-five-degree weather after a late lunch, Ralph and Marvin were laughing about their final during a break between classes. Off somewhere behind them, spectators were clapping at an intramural tennis match.

Wells came by. "It's good to hear laughter during finals."

Ralph chuckled, "I need a new hand after that Philosophy exam!"

Wells smiled. "It'll be worth it come graduation. By then, you'll be fully prepared to enter the work force." He gazed at the knight statues on the facade of the building. "Will you be attending the graduation ceremony next Saturday? The governor will be the guest speaker."

"I hope so. It'll probably be the last time we see Rachel Yards and the others."

Marvin nodded. "What time does graduation start?"

"Noon. . . . How did you meet Ms. Yards and her friends?"

The boys looked at each other. Marvin said, "We heard this energetic girl on the campus radio and had to find out who she was. We asked around. She was kind enough to invite us into her room one night. The boyfriends, Mark and Larry, were there."

Wells asked, "She ever talk to you about secret societies?"

"No."

"Never mention Knights Templar or groups like that?"

Marvin shook his head. "I heard Rachel talk to her friends about a final *paper* on secret societies."

Ralph shrugged. "We did talk about my former roommate, but since the police caught the Woodsman Killer. . . ."

Wells shifted his weight. "Aren't they also interested in that freshman redhead Barbara Quorke?"

Marvin stepped back. "Well, yeah. Since Larry's a reporter for the *University Times*, he spoke to her about her roommate Sarah."

Ralph cleared his throat. "One great thing about Rachel is she's from Jersey. Being from Long Island, I love busting Jersey people, but she's cool."

The wind sent leaves into the air. "Barbara and Steph are both from Philly," Marvin said, "so they have lots in common."

Wells' cell rang. He frowned at the number and clicked the phone shut. "I've often seen the two of you, and Barbara, with them."

Ralph began turning red. "Gee, Professor Wells, Rachel and Steph are gorgeous, and I've had a crush on Rachel since I met her."

Wells smiled. "She's a character."

"I drew a picture of her."

"You what?"

Ralph stuttered, "S-She didn't like it because I gave her a pointy nose."

Wells blushed. "Pointy nose? She's got a big mouth."

Ralph's face was still red. "The first time I met Rachel, she was wearing shorts. Her legs. . . ."

"Young man!"

"Barbara," said Marvin, "had a crush on Mark, but Rachel doesn't take bullshit."

Wells wiped his forehead. "Yes. . . . Well, enough about that. I've also seen how friendly you two are with Dean Sands."

Marvin tapped Ralph's arm. "Sure. We're both interested in constitutional law, and the dean's an expert in that field. Our teachers told us to speak to him."

"Really?"

Ralph rubbed his hands. "We also like how Rachel's into witchcraft."

"Young man." Wells hoisted up his pants. "Witchcraft, black magic, those are very dangerous pursuits, to be avoided at all costs. And this drawing pictures of someone. . .it could be considered stalking. Grounds for disciplinary procedures. You'd better not do something like that again. Do I make myself clear?"

The boys nodded.

Wells grumbled, "Good. Now, study hard for your remaining finals. And remember what I told you. Enjoy the rest of the afternoon." He went off to the tennis match.

Marvin couldn't believe it. "Disciplinary action against you for drawing?"

Ralph shrugged. "We did throw him a few curve balls. And I wasn't kidding about Rachel."

Marvin smacked him in the back of the head. "Come on."


HOURS LATER, listening to Led Zeppelin's "Fool in the Rain" on her iPod, Rachel was dancing up the street, oblivious to the activity in front of the Marshall Complex, where workers were unloading food and other supplies from a catering truck for Saturday's awards dinner. Behind her, near the softball field, Mark was down on one knee, tying his sneaker. Larry and Stephanie were past the truck, hurrying to the cafeteria since it was six-thirty and none of them had eaten. The FCC seminar had run late.

President O'Connor, Drake smoking a cigarette, the security guard from the library, and members of the awards committee were supervising. A discussion started about an order of yams that should have been potatoes. The driver, a Hispanic fellow with a crew-cut, showed the order forms to O'Connor with Drake looking over their shoulders.

Mark was about to catch up to Rachel, but his other shoelace became undone.

Another delivery came down the ramp with frozen goods. Suddenly, the truck began to roll down the street. The ramp fell to the ground. The driver chased after the vehicle.

Larry, Stephanie, and others began shouting, *"Look out!"*

Rachel had her head down, concentrating on her dance steps. When she looked up, she saw a large white truck without a driver careening toward her. She didn't scream, but her face became white and her mouth opened. Hesitating whether to move right or left, she felt a sharp blow near her kidneys and was lifted off her feet. She screamed loud enough to give someone a heart attack. Moments later, she hit the asphalt hard, felt a twinge in her ankle, and something sharp at her forehead. Her iPod shattered.

Mark was lying on top of her. "You all right? That was too close."

She hugged him.

The truck driver leaped onto the seat, edged the vehicle to the curb, and yanked on the emergency brake.

"You're bleeding." Mark ran his knuckles down the right cheek of her face and removed the ear plugs.

People gathered around the two; the security guard was speaking on his walkie-talkie. "Code 5, south of the tennis courts. Repeat. Code 5. Tennis courts." He began yelling at the truck driver. O'Connor grabbed him and whispered something into his ear. He directed students to move back to give the girl room.

On his knees, Mark lifted Rachel to a sitting position. Arm around her shoulders, he gulped, "I'm so sorry."

"Mark." She held his chin. "If you hadn't pushed me out of the way, I'd be dead!"

Stephanie and Larry had by then maneuvered through the crowd to join them. O'Connor asked, "Rachel, are you hurt anywhere?"

She pointed to her feet. "My ankle is killing me, and I may have cracked a rib."

Sirens blasting and lights flashing, an ambulance came down the street, hung a U-turn, and came to a stop. The back door flew open; out came a short guy with glasses. A female EMS volunteer with a ponytail jumped from the side door. The guy did an assessment and said, "Okay, we're going to move you over here." He pointed to the ledge of the vehicle.

Mark said, "We got her." He motioned to Larry. They picked her up and brought her to the ambulance.

"Shit!" She cried out in pain. "My ankle." She was lowered onto the cold aluminum edge of the truck.

Drake and the truck driver continued to argue about the faulty brakes.

The girl with the ponytail leaned toward her. "Are you in pain anywhere?"

Rachel pointed to her side, which the other began to examine.

The short guy said, "The peroxide's going to sting. I suggest you close your eyes."

Then he taped her ankle.

After the ambulance drove away and the crowd left, Rachel used crutches to go to dinner. She had a bandage at the hairline above her right eye. Strands of her hair had been cut away, and an ice pack had been applied to her side. She had been instructed to come to the EMS headquarters the next morning for redressing.

Passing Drake, Stephanie flipped him what remained of Rachel's music box. "Somebody owes her a new iPod."

President O'Connor stopped behind a tree on the side of Temple Hall, hit a pre-recorded number on his cell, and demanded. "Get me Gasso. . . . It's O'Connor. The girl survived another accident. Saturday will be it, I'm sure." He looked around to see if anyone was watching him.

"That's all I needed to hear," said Gasso. "My men and I will be in Suffern tomorrow."

"A ticket will be waiting for you at the door," said the president, glumly eyeing a squirrel that had just run past him.

"Excellent. Take care of yourself."

"If anything happens to me, speak to the girl directly." O'Connor turned off his phone and dragged himself back to the deliveries.

At 11:00 P.M., IN THE MONKS' MEETING ROOM in the basement of Knights Hall, the master pounded a gavel on the round wooden table. "Another failed attempt on her life." One of three faxes started beeping behind him on workbenches that also contained five humming computers, printers, four phones, a small copier, a scanner, three laptops and a DVD-VCR player plugged into a ten inch TV. Above that equipment hung reproductions of three paintings: *Battle of the Nude Gods, Robbers Hanged from a Tree,* and *Death of Socrates.*

The four other monks nodded somberly.

The master stared at them. "The search of their rooms for the documents failed to turn up a thing." Glancing at the maps of the campus, the tunnels, Suffern, Rockland County, and America, he continued, "We have to assume they have the documents in their possession. They probably gave copies to those three freshmen. If anything happened to them, Rachel and her friends would scream so loud, Albany would hear it."

A shorter monk sitting next to the master asked, "Think they've already gone public with the info?"

The master shook his head. "If they had, we'd have known it by now. I should've gone up to the tower myself and brought them down here to hang with the others. I've notified the Secret Brotherhood about our problem."

"And?"

"And!" He shook the table to the point of rattling the chandelier above them. "We're going to end up like Emerson, Schmidt, and Cunningham. We're one of the main operation centers that keeps an elite group alive in America, and it may be compromised here because of one crazy child from Jersey!"

The fax finished beeping.

He pounded the gavel again. "Why was only one man on patrol when those four troublemakers traveled through the tunnels?" Before anyone answered, he grumbled, "All the missed opportunities to stop them! The only thing we have to show for it is her heels and a notebook from the first encounter." He gestured to a small table by the near wall below the Knights Templar's symbol of two knights on one horse. "Edward Knights and Joe Temple are probably turning over in their graves because a single girl is destroying their university."

One of the monks said, "At least she's been a beautiful opponent."

"True." The master agreed. "But, come Saturday, we strike her down!"

# CHAPTER 23

ITH HIS BACK TO THE MORNING SUN on Friday, Mark flung a Frisbee to Larry on the grass in front of the seven-floor gothic Swords Hall.

Larry returned it, spinning it so it dipped at Mark's shins, and the girls cheered.

Further down, six guys and girls were also tossing Frisbees.

"Hello, ladies," said Dean Sands, looking sharp in a dark suit and sunglasses. He had come from the library. "You two comfortable?"

"Yes. Would you like to join us?" Rachel patted the middle cushion of the couch they were sitting on. Moments before, the guys had vacated those seats.

"No, thanks. . . . How did you get this furniture out here?"

"The guys," said Stephanie, "were sweet enough to carry it out."

"I see." He put his briefcase down. "Who gave you permission to bring it outdoors?"

Rachel shrugged. "With my injuries, they wanted me to be comfortable." Her right ankle was still taped, and she had an ice pack on her side. A bandage covered half her forehead. A pair of crutches was leaning against the side of the couch.

He fixed his tie. "That's very thoughtful of them. What makes you so special?"

Stephanie raised her hand. "Dean Sands, Rachel was injured on school property through the negligence of a catering company hired by the university. She was almost killed. . .and a lawsuit isn't out of the question."

He nodded. "When you're finished having fun, make sure the couch is returned. . .and this will be the last time."

"Yes, sir." Rachel smiled. "What, by the way, was wrong with the truck?"

He picked up his briefcase. "Old brakes. The incline was enough to cause them to slip out of gear."

"Help!" the guys yelled. The Frisbee landed near the couch.

In a huff, Sands tossed it back.

The girls clapped. "Good throw, sir!"

"Thanks. I played basketball and baseball in college. Keep in shape by swimming now, and walking everywhere. I get around." His eyebrows rose. "Rachel! Now that I'm getting a good look at you, you seem to have been through a war. Will you be able to attend tomorrow night's dinner?"

"You better believe it. My gown arrived last night." She turned and felt pain shoot through her. "I've been fighting two ugly bitches, medieval characters, and other forces for weeks, and I'm still going like the Energizer Bunny. You sure you don't want to join us?"

He frowned. "No. I must be leaving."

Once Sands entered York Hall, Stephanie laughed. "He could've sat on the documents."

"He'll have to wait until tomorrow." Rachel smiled.

Two hours later, near the doors of the cafeteria inside the Marshall Complex, Rachel said, "Steph and I have to go to the ladies room."

Mark pecked her on the cheek. "Okay. We'll wait here."

They headed toward an archway between a bulletin board covered by flyers and the book store.

Coming up the five steps, the Tree and Fatso smiled. "Rachel! We were glad to hear Mark saved you from that truck. It would have been a horrible way to die."

Rachel sighed.

Passing them, Theresa laughed. "Too bad you didn't bust your jaw. That way you would've been quiet for months."

Rachel shoved the crutch at Fatso's knee, forcing her to the floor and, at the same time, pushing Theresa off balance. She stumbled into an unsuspecting freshman.

"You *bitch!*" Frowning, teeth clenched, Theresa charged at them with arms raised.

"Wait a minute!" David leaped up the stairs from the men's room. "You're going to attack Rachel? Can't you see she's handicapped?"

Stephanie waved Mark and Larry off. "Thanks, David."

David escorted the two girls out the building.

Five minutes later as Rachel and Stephanie were drinking from a water fountain, Barbara sailed down the steps and asked, "What's up?"

Stephanie said, "Not much. We're about to have lunch. Want to join us?"

Barbara nodded. "Absolutely." She waited for Rachel to wipe her mouth to add, "When Ralph and Marvin told me what happened to you, I wanted to cry. The four of you should be commended for what you're doing."

Rachel rested on the crutches. "Thanks. Don't get yourself so worked up about it. I'm still in one piece."

Barbara shook her head. "Shows how *desperate* those bastards are."

Mark stared at Rachel.

She raised her eyebrows.

"Excuse me, Rachel." Barbara stepped closer to her. "I'd also like to apologize to you for the way I've been behaving toward Mark. It was a stupid case of puppy love. He's your guy. Don't ever lose him. And you've got more guts than some of these so-called men on campus."

"Well, thank you very much. That's very sweet of you. It took a lot to say that."

Barbara grabbed Rachel's hand. "Is there anything I can do to make up for it?"

The seniors turned to each other. "As a matter of fact, there is."

AFTER LUNCH, BARBARA WAS SITTING alone on a sunlit bench near Temple Hall, the wind blowing through her hair, when she saw O'Connor open the bronze doors. She began to sniffle.

He came over. "Why are you crying? What's wrong?"

She wiped away tears. "...Today's my last day on campus. My parents will be picking me up. I said goodbye to my friends, but not to my roommate...."

He clasped his hands. "What's your name?"

"Barbara Quorke."

He straightened up. "Who's your roommate?"

She wiped her nose with a tissue. "Sarah Appleton."

The smugness left his face. "I'm. . .I'm so sorry, Ms. Quorke. We were all terribly upset by her disappearance. It was awful that such a young life was cut short. Hopefully, the capture of that vicious killer brought some closure."

She nodded. "It has, but. . .I didn't get a chance to say goodbye to her, and we, well, you see, we weren't good riends. . . ."

"There, there." He patted her shoulder. He removed a business card from his wallet and wrote down his cell number. "If you need to talk more, feel free to call me."

"Thanks."

He asked, "Are your finals over?"

"Yes." She took a deep breath. "I still have to pack."

He rubbed his wrinkled cheek. "My grandmother used to say, 'When you're upset, think of happy thoughts and smell the flowers, which frees the mind of sorrow.'" He motioned behind her. "There's plenty of 'em right there."

She got up. "Thanks again, sir."

They went in separate directions.

Two hours later, the president's cell rang. "O'Connor."

"'*Origins of Knights University, by Gordon Cunningham.*' If you want to hear more, meet me at the duck pond at six-thirty."

"Who is this?"

"Harvard professor, G.I.C." The line went dead.

He rested his forehead on his palms. The silence of the office offered no solutions. He hit a pre-recorded number on his cell. "Get me Gasso." After a couple of minutes that seemed like an hour, Gasso picked up the phone.

"They have the proof," said O'Connor. "One of them called me to arrange a meeting. I was right. Tomorrow will be D-Day."

"The moment things go down Saturday, you notify me!"

O'Connor shut off his phone, looked at his belongings, and mumbled, "I'm getting too old for this."

As the long sunset spread across the campus, ushering in a breeze and turning the clouds a reddish-pink, O'Connor was rising from a bench at the pond when he saw a person approach him. "*Stephanie?* I was expecting Rachel."

She smiled. "Cooler heads prevailed. Besides, she's nursing her ankle."

He placed his hands on his hips. "When did you get the— uh, the documents?"

She moved around him to sit down. "Last Saturday, close to midnight. We're going to expose everything at the Awards Dinner. Friends of ours will be bringing copies to the *Times* and *News*."

He joined her on the bench. "End of an era."

She crossed her legs. "Besides his sick in-laws, what brought Cunningham here?"

He chuckled at a squirrel fighting the ducks over the pieces of bread he had thrown into the water. "Gordon had written a number of papers on the Revolutionary War. His expertise on that subject gave him a lot of visibility. His colleagues loved him."

Stephanie asked, "Why the church tower?"

"Great hiding spot—and a place of faith."

"Why has this secret society been allowed to run this school for a hundred years?"

He shook his head. "Steph, you're young, so I forgive your innocence. For at least two thousand years, there have been secret societies on this planet. Religious-military, like the Knights Templar, and politically oriented, like the Rosicrucians. When America was discovered, half of Europe scrambled to seize possession of it. England prevailed in the end. The Revolution broke that stranglehold, but the leaders of the colonies were Freemasons who still had ties with European trading interests and families like the Rothschilds. Therefore, we developed on the English model, politically, socially, economically. . . ."

She kicked a rock into the pond. "America doesn't have a monarchy." The bright red reflection from the windows of the nearby buildings made her squint.

"True." He cleared his throat. "But it *does* have an aristocracy. And like most other countries, it's a pyramid. Rich elite at the top, masses in the middle and bottom. Most people wouldn't admit that, but I have nothing to lose anymore. The members of our group want to maintain that status quo, and one way was the establishment of certain colleges and universities. These 'monks,' as you and your friends choose to call them, answer to a higher authority whose mission on Earth is beyond your understanding. You were probably only four years old at the time, but the crash of 1987 was not a surprise to them: They cashed in on it. The Dot.com crash of 2000, by comparison, was pure stupidity."

She adjusted her glasses. "Weren't they afraid people were going to discover their operation here. . .and have they no guilt about the killings?"

He buttoned his jacket. "Steph, people will do anything to maintain power and their web. I'm not talking about the Internet, which stretches around the globe and is as interconnected as life itself."

The sky was turning a deep blue-gray.

She asked, "How did the professor hide the documents?"

"Tools from the supply room, and he used rope to get up there.

How do you think he was hanged?"

She shivered the way she had when she saw *The Amityville Horror* alone one stormy night during high school. She hadn't listened to her parents' warnings. For weeks, she'd thought she heard voices calling, *Get out.* She looked around, noticing they were alone. "Stuff like this goes on across the country?"

He nodded. "Who was brave enough to go up to the weathervane?"

She tilted her head at him. "How come none of the monks went for the documents?"

He smiled. "They became an urban legend, like a killer with a knife in the back seat of a vehicle or a drunken girl at a party who passes out and, later on, wakes up in a pile of ice only to discover one of her kidneys missing." He sniffed. "Some figured no one would search for Gordon's scribbles. Others didn't believe they existed, or didn't realize how much material was up there. A search party found nothing after five minutes and left. When I was told about them, my fate was already sealed, so I didn't concern myself about the matter at all until Rachel got involved.

"What a great rumor it became! Classified documents about a secret society forming this college funded by the Mafia, hidden in the church tower. It seemed no different from legends about other universities. Witches terrorizing schools in New England. Ghosts of Confederate soldiers haunting Southern campuses. Places in the Midwest built on Indian burial grounds." He glanced sidelong at her. "Just remember, Stephanie, as they say in baseball, it's not over till it's over."

In the shadow of a nearby building, a cigarette fell to the pavement, and footsteps vanished northward.

# CHAPTER 24

RACHEL WAS DABBING PERFUME behind her ears when she heard a knock. She paused in an unaccustomed moment of trepidation before she put the bottle down on the top of her dresser and called out, "Who is it?"

"Mark."

"Coming, sweetie." Barefoot, she unlocked the chain and let him in. "Can you zip me up?" She closed the door.

He did.

She asked, "How do I look?" She spun around for him. Her thick-strapped black evening gown showed off her cleavage, and a slit revealed much of one leg.

He latched onto her waist. "Rachel!"

"Easy! My *side!*" she gasped. "Mark. Calm down."

He started sucking on her neck. "Can we. . .skip the dinner?"

"Mark!" She felt his hands on her rear end. "Control yourself."

"Sorry." He stood up. "You look fabulous. . . . How's your ankle?"

She smiled. "Better. Two dances, though, and I'll probably need ice on it." She straightened his tie. "After the dinner, we'll have some fun." They embraced and kissed non-stop for a minute, then gazed into each other's eyes. "Have the stuff?"

He nodded.

She leaned on him to put on her heels, turned off the lights, and kissed him some more. She whispered, "We'd better go." They left arm in arm.

They were soon inside the brightly lit ballroom. Leaning on his back, Rachel whistled. "What a setup!"

Thirty-five round tables in white cloths, each set for ten, with red roses in the center and numbers in picture frames; waiters and waitresses serving salad and pouring cold water, streamed from a door behind the stage in the far corner of the room.

Mark pointed. "There's our parents, talking by our table."

Rachel said, "I also see Larry and his father. Steph must've gone to the bathroom."

Mark cleared his throat. "Larry's mother's visiting his aunt in the hospital. She had a stroke. My brother's away on business in California for two weeks."

Conversations were louder than Rod Stewart's "Maggie May" on the sound system. In the near corner, O'Connor was talking to the governor and mayor.

Wells tested the sound equipment on the stage. A small drum set, keyboards, wires, amps, and three microphones sat in the rear. Below and in front, a table covered by the awards and a gray apron, with *Knights University* in black, faced the audience. At the edge of the stage, people were dancing. Gray and white balloons hung from the ceiling. Banners featured *Annual Knights Awards Dinner 2005.*

Rachel smiled. "It's cool to see men dressed in suits and tuxedos, and I love the gowns. I must say, Mark, you look very sharp in blue."

He blushed. "Rach, shouldn't we say hi to our parents?"

She shifted to one side. "You can go. I see someone I have to say hello to." They kissed. She seemed to float past tables then spun around when she came upon Dean Sands. "Hello, sir. How are you? You look handsome in that tuxedo."

He lifted her hands. "Rachel, you're gorgeous, but forgive me." He kissed her fingertips. "I'm wanted by the stage." He continued in that direction.

"Rachel!" Stephanie hugged her. "That gown is awesome! No wonder you wouldn't show me what you were going to wear tonight. You look great in black."

"Thank you."

"Rach." Stephanie motioned to the plump, six-two man next to her, whose white hair matched his dinner jacket. "You remember my father?"

"Of course." Rachel extended her hand but received a bear hug instead. "Great seeing you again, sir."

His loud voice complemented his behavior. "The pleasure is all mine. I'll leave you two young ladies to talk." He lumbered off to his table.

Rachel smiled. "I don't remember him being so aggressive."

Stephanie chuckled. "You weren't wearing *that*. What did Mark think of it?"

"He wanted to skip dinner."

"See some skin and lose control."

"Your outfit's beautiful."

"Thanks." Stephanie's red gown had sleeves, a V neck, and a slit to her knee.

Rachel asked, "How's your mother?"

"Still recovering from that hip surgery. My sister's taking care of her."

Rachel nodded. "My brothers won't be here tonight either, but they're coming to the graduation."

Passing them, Drake said, "Evening, ladies. You both look stupendous."

Stephanie leaned toward her. "You're turning lots of heads."

Rachel flipped her hand at the wrist. "Don't be silly, it's you. Where were you and your father coming from?"

"Talking to Loom about stocks."

They were interrupted when President O'Connor approached the microphone. "Good evening, ladies and gentlemen! Can I have your attention?" The noise level fell by half. "Please. May I have your attention?" It came to a halt. "Welcome to the seventy-fifth annual Knights Awards Dinner." The place erupted into applause and cheers. "On behalf of the university, I would like to welcome the governor, the mayor, honored guests, the administration, the faculty, alumni, seniors, and your families. We have a full program tonight, so please take your seats. Salad has already been served. Thank you."

"The governor." Stephanie snapped her fingers. "What's the plan?"

"After the main course," Rachel whispered, "the governor and mayor will give speeches. Then come the awards. I'm the ninth winner. During my speech, I'll call the three of you up. At one point, Ralph's supposed to call. He was so excited about helping, we forgot about our cell numbers."

Stephanie shrugged. "My father's friend is at table twenty."

"Ladies." Wells looked at them. "Save me a dance."

"We will." Rachel motioned Stephanie to the center of the room.

At table eighteen, after hugs and kisses, they discussed attending Rutgers' graduate school to continue in communications and their internship at the radio station. The four told their parents about the FCC seminar, the trips, and future ones like an upcoming game at Yankee Stadium.

WHILE THE PASTA COURSE was being served, Dean Sands approached the microphone to a round of applause. "Thank you, and good evening. There is much to be proud about tonight. Soon, over thirty seniors will be receiving awards in academics, athletics, and extracurricular activities like the radio station." Plenty of noise came from table eighteen. "Our graduates will be heading toward such fields as investment banking, accounting, law schools, the media, computer programming, civil engineering, and government. A graduate from '02 will soon clerk for Supreme Court Justice Antonin Scalia." Ohhs and ahhs rose from the audience. He went on to explain the school's budget was on target. The university was receiving sizable donations from alumni, foundations, trusts, and companies, but more was always welcome. He emphasized, "We remain committed to academic excellence by retaining dedicated faculty like Professors Drake, Wells, and Loom, to name but a few. I'm also proud to announce that, come fall, the largest freshman class in Knights' history will be attending this school. Thank you." He bowed at the reaction.

Wiping sauce off his mouth, Mr. Yards asked, "Rachel, I meant to ask you—why'd you ask your brothers for the rope?" His features were almost identical to his daughter's: dark hair, though with a touch of gray throughout, angled eyebrows, brown eyes, a round nose, and a flat chin.

She raised her eyebrows. "We. . .had a tug-of-war between the residents of Clarks and Swords Hall."

He nodded.

Mark said, "Mrs. Yards, when Rachel showed me a picture of her brothers, I didn't think she was related to them. They have rounder faces and a much lighter complexion. And she has brown eyes and hair black as the ace of clubs."

The dirty-blonde, blue-eyed woman laughed. "She's like her father in many ways." She brushed off a look from both.

Mr. Lexington remarked, "Mark's a combination of Samantha and me, without the dirt on his face."

Mark frowned.

Mr. Moore, sporting a mustache on a boxy face like his son, chuckled, "Facial hair is a good thing when you're losing it up here." He touched his receding hairline.

Rachel ran her fingers over Mark's goatee.

"Rachel!" Her mother glared. "Not at the dinner table."

Mr. and Mrs. Lexington turned to each other in silence.

Mr. Brooks' voice made everyone turn to him. "I think it's splendid the four of you will stick together. Going to Rutgers New Brunswick for graduate school is wonderful. Soon after that, we'll be hearing you all deejay on FM!"

Everyone lifted wine glasses.

The band started playing "Satisfaction."

The four got up to dance. Shaking next to Rachel, Stephanie asked, "Who's the guy in the gray suit, talking to O'Connor?"

Rachel, moving from side to side, shrugged. "Someone from the Gambinos?"

"Or one of the higher authority?"

Rachel shook her head and moved up closer to Mark. "Sorry for touching your goatee."

He whispered in her ear. "Your mother is making my parents uncomfortable."

Rachel frowned. "I'd skip family parties. Mom would never join us camping. I'd go to Giants' games with Dad. I wasn't feminine enough for her."

Four songs later, they were at the table again, eating steak or salmon. O'Connor and Wells stopped by to say a few words.

When the band returned for a second set, everyone from that table began to dance except Mr. Lexington and Mr. Moore, who were smoking cigars in the far corner. In the middle of the first song, a Mexican waiter tapped Rachel on the shoulder and whispered to her, "Excuse me, Ms. Yards. There's a call for you from a Ralph Ford on the phone in the hallway."

She smiled. "I was expecting it. . . . Thanks."

He disappeared among the moving bodies.

Her parents asked, "What's up?"

She pointed. "I have a phone call in the hallway."

They nodded.

She began to limp off the packed dance floor.

The others did not see her go. In the far corner, Lexington, Moore, and other fathers had by then produced a thick cloud of smoke.

Nearing table eighteen, Rachel felt dizzy. She grabbed the chair she'd been sitting in and drank a glass of water. After a deep breath, she limped to the door. When she stepped into the hallway, she couldn't believe how dark, and how much cooler, it was. The clicking of her heels was the only sound. She turned left. She rubbed her arms. An exit sign near the ceiling guided her to the payphone. The commuter lounge was deserted. A good distance later, she turned left to the phone. Next to her stood an emergency door. The receiver was on top of the black Verizon machine. "Hello? It's Rachel. . . .Hello? . . . Ralph?"

She felt a cold, sharp object between her shoulder blades, and an eerie voice growled, "Put the receiver down."

She did and started crying.

The attacker covered her mouth and slid the knife down her back. He used the point of the blade to unzip her dress. Gliding the knife up her back from the edge of the gown, he murmured, "What beauty, but so vulnerable."

The sound of his voice, and the smell of his breath, made her stop crying. A gleam of recognition entered her eyes.

The monk put the knife below her chin. "Resist, and I'll slit your throat."

Tears formed in her eyes again.

Four sets of footsteps converged in the corner.

She began to moan, stiff as a board.

The monk whispered, "We're taking you for a ride." He lifted up his robe to place the knife in a holder attached to his leg. Putting his other hand on the back of her head, he moved to her side.

Meantime, another monk had bent down to grab her ankles from behind, and a third, shorter, seized her thighs. Yet another grabbed her waist. The tallest man reached around her shoulders to pin her arms. They lifted her off her feet as she began to struggle. The lead monk guided them to the door. He pushed open the emergency door with his shoulder without setting off the alarm. They were soon heading down the first of three flights of stairs.

When Mr. and Mrs. Yards returned to the table, Mark asked, "Where's Rachel?"

Her father told him about the waiter.

Mark shouted, "*Steph*! *Larry*! Rachel hasn't returned! Get O'Connor!"

"What's wrong?" Mr. Yards exclaimed.

Stephanie pointed in the direction of the stage. "There he is, coming toward us."

"Rachel's missing!" Mark yelled, almost bumping into him at the next table.

O'Connor grabbed a walkie-talkie from his jacket. "Ducktail! Repeat, *Ducktail*!"

Instantly, the man in the gray suit, who had a marine hair cut, a high forehead, and a thick neck, came rushing over. "Ducktail!" He barked into his walkie-talkie. "Do we know where they've taken her?" He had a dire expression on his clean-shaven face.

O'Connor shook his head. "Probably the basement of the old library in Knights Hall!"

The guy with the walkie-talkie was already nodding. "Old library Knights Hall basement. *Out!*"

The parents gathered around.

The chief came running to the group and shook Mr. Brooks' hand.

O'Connor slipped a sheet of paper into the pocket of the broad-shouldered man with the round head, whose hazel eyes had seen much wickedness in his time. He looked at the list of names.

O'Connor shouted, "Ernie!" to the African American security guard near the stage.

The stocky man's wide face was immediately alert. "Yes, sir?"

"Follow me!" O'Connor rushed out the door with the others in tow.

Mark yelled, "Mom! Wait here with Mrs. Yards."

At the telephone, the guy in the gray suit shone a flashlight on the floor and bent down to pick up something glittering in the light.

Stephanie gasped, "That's Rachel's earring."

"This way." O'Connor pushed open the door. No alarm sounded.

Ernie pulled out his flashlight and spoke into his walkie-talkie. "Get me a detail at the old library." He followed Mr. Moore.

Stephanie waved her father on. "Go. *Go.*" Before she ran down the stairs, she kicked off her heels.

The five monks had meanwhile bashed through the basement labeled and plunged into the tunnels. Rachel was struggling like hell.

Outside, Suffern and state police, four-door sedans with FBI and Treasury agents, and army vehicles with armed men in full uniform, were converging on Knights Hall and the Marshall Complex.

Deep in the tunnel, the master said, "You interfering bitch! You may have blown this wide open, but it will cost you your life."

Rachel continued to struggle.

Turning left in the tunnel, the man O'Connor had been speaking with earlier used his walkie-talkie. "We're on the move to the old library in Knights Hall. Out." He pulled a handgun from his jacket.

Mr. Yards asked, "O'Connor. Who the hell is *he*?"

O'Connor, running, kept his flashlight straight ahead. "Never mind that."

Mr. Brooks' voice echoed throughout the passageway. "What the hell *is* this place?"

From the rear, Stephanie shouted, "Dad, welcome to the world of secret societies!"

In the dark basement of Knights Hall, the five monks halted in front of a gargoyle on the wall. The master twisted the creature's mouth, which hissed open a portion. "Time's ticking away, sweetheart."

She groaned, but when the wall closed, her life passed before her eyes. She remembered the first time she drove up with her family to the college. Everyone was in awe. Returning from camping trips, she'd seen the university when they stopped in Suffern for dinner and was intrigued by its medieval look. She bit the master's hand.

"You *fuck*!"

The man with the handgun asked, "How much further?"

Feeling his chest, O'Connor gasped, "Not much. We'll go through the weapons closet."

"The what?"

In the old library, candles surrounded the table Melvin and Sarah had shared in death. The men flung Rachel on her back and tied her wrists and ankles to posts.

She grunted in pain.

Tying a rope around her mouth, the master said, "You wouldn't stop despite the warnings. Now there's no way out."

She kept rolling back and forth on the table.

HAND ON THE GARGOYLE'S MOUTH, O'Connor kept waving everyone in. "Keep going. Keep going." He held out his hand to Stephanie, who was breathing as if she was going to pass out. "Gimme your hand, Steph."

On the other side of a bookshelf, Gasso heard people humming and someone moaning. He saw yellow light and smelled burning wax. Behind him, he heard footsteps and heavy breathing, to his left other footsteps.

The master raised the knife and aimed it at Rachel's throat. "Say your prayers."

"*Freeze!* FBI! Put that knife down!" Agent Gasso ordered, pointing the handgun and flashlight at them. ". . .Step away from the table!"

Twenty-five FBI SWAT agents, using night goggles and carrying machine guns, swarmed into the area. They shouted, "Step away from the table! On your *knees*! *Now*!"

Gasso ordered, "Get *away* from her!"

The monk dropped the knife to the floor.

O'Connor yelled, "It's over, John! It's over. I'm turning state's evidence."

The lights were turned on.

The SWAT team had the monks on their knees, unmasked, and handcuffed. Others were cutting the rope from Rachel's limbs.

The group was shocked to see Sands at the head of the table, along with Drake, Loom, Heglan, and Sergeant Dolan.

Stephanie grumbled, "May all of you go to hell."

Gasso stood over Sands. "You're under arrest for murder, attempted murder, kidnapping, money laundering, torture, and blackmail. Get him outta here." Two SWAT men took him away.

Two others helped Rachel off the table. She collapsed onto her knees against Mark's chest.

A SWAT member announced, "Agent Gasso. The Marshall Complex is secure. A Professor Wells had been cooperating with the U.S. Treasury since last month. And a chief of police from PA also helped in the investigation. The governor's been escorted to his car. The assistant dean has taken over the party."

"Good." Gasso wiped his forehead. "Take these sons-of-bitches away."

# CHAPTER 25

B ELOW AN AERIAL VIEW OF THE SCHOOL, the *Sunday New York Times* ran a cover story headlined *Scandal at Knights University* above a bulleted list that read: *Ruled by Secret Society. Financed by Mafia Money. Tales of Murder and Torture. FBI Investigates.*

Coming from the Marshall Complex, passing Temple Hall that warm evening, Mark read from the newspaper, "Senior Rachel Yards. . . ."

Rachel pointed. "President O'Connor."

O'Connor had been walking from Temple Hall. He smiled. "Rachel. Mark. How are you two doing?"

She put her arm around Mark. "Better. Thanks."

"Mr. President," Mark asked, "where does the university go from here?"

O'Connor looked up at the darkening sky. "Well, there have already been ten phone calls from parents of students in the incoming class about withdrawing and going with their other acceptances. The Admissions Office has to develop new recruiting strategies.

And there's the bad press. The six o'clock news will be running a special bulletin on universities starting Monday. We'll make the cover of *Newsweek* and *Time* next week. The admin is working side by side with the FBI, and the Justice and Education Departments. Congress will soon begin a full-scale investigation into this matter. Finance will probably find itself strapped for a while, but this place will survive." He chuckled, "It's ironic, but the History Department has been thinking about offering classes on secret societies in the fall for the past few months."

Mark laughed. "Rachel's qualified to teach that."

O'Connor cleared his throat. "The feds have been sealing the tunnels and clearing out the secret chambers. Agent Gasso approached me after Melvin disappeared. Conspiracy theorists, followers of secret societies, believers in class divisions are having a field day." He took a deep breath. "Rachel, you freed the souls of the ghosts. They are no longer trapped in this dimension. And you brought down that monster Sands. You should be proud of yourself."

Mark hugged her.

Rachel asked, "How did Dean Sands become the leader of K & T?"

O'Connor crossed his arms. "He was the most inspired of the group, and his great-grandfather married Joe Temple's sister, Joan. Sands and company paid the Woodsmen Killer to take responsibility for the deaths of Sarah and Melvin." He shook his head. "I tried to scare you, Rachel—the mask on the bench, the falling encyclopedias at the library—but there was no stopping you."

Rachel nodded. "I've always been a fighter. My mother and I used to fight tooth and nail, but this situation has brought us closer.

What I've been through has changed her attitude to me. We had a long talk earlier. Heck, The Tree and Fatso even apologized to me!"

"Excellent!" O'Connor clapped. "You're not going to Shields Bar?"

Turning to Mark, she said, "We're going to have a quiet celebration."

O'Connor blushed. "Well, then, I'll have a drink for the two of you."